SANTA MAYBE

Holidays in Lake Point 1

Sarah Cass

Sensual Romance

Sarah Cass
www.authorsarahcass.com

Divine Roses Ink Publishing
www.divinerosesink.com

A Divine Roses Ink Book
Sensual Romance

Santa Maybe
Copyright © 2013 Sarah Cass
Second E-book Publication: September 2015
First E-book Publication: December 2013

Cover design by Sarah Cass
Edited by Megan Koenen
Proofread by Renee Waring
All cover art and logo copyright © 2013 by Sarah Cass

PUBLISHER
Divine Roses Ink
http://www.divinerosesink.com

Books by Sarah Cass

The Tribe Series
The Tribe
The Wolf
The Chief
The Raven
The Dominion Falls Series
Changing Tracks
Derailed
Dark Territory
Runaway Train
Home Signal
The Lake Point Series
Santa, Maybe
Deep-Fried Sweethearts
Stalled Independence
Witch Way
A Thorough Thanksgiving
Eve's New Year
Heartstrings & Hockey Pucks
Luck of the Cowgirl
Stars, Stripes & Motorbikes
Free Falling
Love for Hire
Stand Alone Novels
Masked Hearts
Leap

Dedication

To my two kids with Cystic Fibrosis, Denver and
Kennedy.
You are two of the strongest people I have ever
met.
You inspire me daily.

And to all the children with Cystic Fibrosis in the
world.
Once this was unbeatable, but every day they're a
step closer.
Be strong.
Survive.

To the Cystic Fibrosis Foundation.
Thank you.
Thank you.
Thank you.

http://cff.org

Chapter One

Alan wove through the crowd, guiding his mom by the arm. Every year Lake Point threw a festival for the tree lighting ceremony and every year it was the same. Only difference now was somehow they'd added a skating rink in the middle of the street.

Vendors and stay-at-home-mom's that did crafts had booths up with their wares. Everything and anything that ranged from tacky, odd clothes for dogs, up to expensive and elaborate wood carvings was sold. But nothing being sold was worth their time, and they needed to head to The Midway and the booth out front for some warm cocoa for his mom, Dorothy, nicknamed Dotty.

At a smack to his hand, he stopped short and frowned. "It's too crowded. We can go over there and rest," he said.

"Too crowded? This from the big New York City boy?" his mother said, smiling at him. Gray hair, with sprinkles of black still scattered throughout, shimmered in the street lights. She adjusted her glasses. "I happen to enjoy walking along the tents and checking out the wares. Many of these items are homemade, you know."

"I know, Mom. Your house is overflowing with junk from these places."

"Junk? Every piece is beautiful, and helped someone earn a little extra money." A stern pinch wrinkled the thin flesh around her lips. "Why don't you go see if some of your friends can play?"

"I'm not sixteen anymore. I don't 'play'."

"It's a damn shame too. Now go on, Alan. I can take care of myself. I'm not an invalid just yet."

Alan hesitated even as she shooed him off with her hands. Despite her claims to not be an invalid, and her spirited brush off, he still worried about her. In the twenty years since he'd left town with Ivy she'd turned down every bit of help he'd offered for her financially. Ever since his father's well-earned diagnosis of liver cancer, his mom had been working to make sure everything was 'fine', as she'd always done Alan's whole life, most notably when his sister Amy had died. Now that his father was finally going to kick the bucket, she'd been distraught. In fact, tonight was the first time Alan had seen her relax since he'd arrived.

It was the only reason he'd come home, to help her through his dad's passing. His role was to help make sure she was financially ready and knowledgeable enough to handle the bills, make final funeral arrangements, and then get the hell out of Dodge.

"I hear there is entertainment over by the food carts. You remember where they keep those during the celebration, don't you?" She smiled and quirked a brow until it disappeared under the fringe of hair above her glasses.

"Nothing has changed in twenty years, Mom. I feel like I stepped into a damn time machine and came back to the scene of the crime."

"No more of that talk. Go. Try to remember how to have fun."

"Don't buy too much, Mom. Not unless you're willing to use that account I set up for you." He sighed when she scoffed and disappeared into a tent full of carved wood knick-knacks. Years ago he'd set up the account for her, and she'd never touched a dime. Since then, between interest and his monthly deposits, she had a good-sized nest egg. If only she'd just use it.

He scratched the back of his head and ran his finger along the inside of his starched shirt collar. The town square of Lake Point, New York was bustling full of people far less dressed up than he was. He'd refused to change his style just because he'd come back to the small town from New York City, and part of him was regretting it as his well-cut wool coat, and finely tailored suit stuck out like a sore thumb.

As per his mom's request he'd come home for Thanksgiving and planned to stay on until around New Years, unless he could come up with an excuse to go back to the city before then. As much as he wanted to help his mom, being back in this small town felt a little suffocating.

He started to weave through the crowd again, toward the sound of music being forced through a speaker; the tinny tunes of Christmas were accompanied by out of synch taps. *Oh goody, they've added dancing children to the fun-fest,* he thought bitterly. All he wanted to do was get a coffee and sit and wait while his mom shopped. If tradition held true, and he knew it did, in another two hours they'd finally light all the Christmas lights via a rather realistic Santa impersonator and the town would divide. Half would return home and wait until the light show was less crowded, the other half would fill the car-path through the local park for the light show.

Every year it was the same thing, for as far back as he could remember. Nothing changed in this town, and that was why he refused to talk about the town or the changes his mom claimed were happening. The changes were all in her head, after all. And it made him want none of it.

"Alan? Alan Richards?" He recognized the voice a moment before he saw an extremely short and perky blonde bounce down the courthouse grounds and hop off the ledge onto the sidewalk. Her hair tied up in a ponytail with a festive ribbon, Mary Powell could have stepped right out of their senior yearbook. It wasn't until she sprang right up and hugged him tight that he saw signs she'd aged as he had. Tiny wrinkles rimmed her eyes when she smiled. "Never thought I'd see you again."

"Makes two of us." Alan chuckled to soften the words of truth. "Sometimes responsibilities win out. How are you? Haven't seen you in twenty years."

"I'm great! Went to SUNY, got my degree. I'm teaching at the high school now. I'm also the cheerleading coach."

"From head cheerleader to coach. Imagine that." He let the droll tone flow out, glad she laughed at it. "You haven't changed a bit."

"Unlike some people." She plucked at his lapel. "Nice. I'd heard you made it big. Not that any of us are surprised."

He shrugged, "I do well enough. Listen, it's great to see you and all, but I wanted to go and—"

"Let me guess. You want to see Ivy?"

Ice rushed through his veins and he pinched his brows together. "I'm sorry. Did you say Ivy? You can't mean Ivy Nowell."

"Well who else would I mean?"

"But she's in the city." She had to be in the city. Last time he'd seen her had been eight years ago, but she'd still been at the peak of her career. Despite their split, he'd gone to every opening and closing to see her. But then eight years ago her bio disappeared off the website; her name dropped off every program at her ballet company. His attendance of a few opening and closing nights after had only confirmed her absence. He'd wondered what had happened to her, but despite not knowing that, he knew for certain the last thing she'd do was come back here. They'd left this place happily behind them together right after they finished high school to make their mark in New York, and to live their lives together.

Mary's ponytail bobbed as she shook her head. "No, she's not. Hasn't been for about eight years. How could you not know that? When she returned without you, we assumed you'd split, maybe divorced."

"Divorced? But we..." He trailed off before he revealed too much. They'd split years before, well before they'd managed to get married. Why would Mary assume that? Was Ivy really here? And what had she told them? "Where is she?"

Curiosity struck a spark in Mary's brown eyes and she leaned up toward him. "I always wondered why she didn't talk about you anymore."

"I asked where she was, Mary." He set his hands on his hips and frowned. "I find it hard to believe that she came back here."

"Go see for yourself. She's over there right now." Mary waved toward the stage where the tinny music echoed from. The music came from the *Nutcracker,* the opening party scene as he recalled from seeing Ivy in the show many times. "My daughter's the one on the far right. Isn't she just adorable in her costume?"

Alan spun around to look. The girl she pointed out looked very much like a young Mary, right down to still having baby fat. Downright adorable, but she wasn't what really caught his eye. At the edge of the stage, just out of sight from anyone looking dead-on from the audience, was Ivy.

Pink shimmering point shoes, simple white tights and skirt, topped with a white leotard that appeared to have sequins or rhinestones on it that caught in the lights with each of her movements. Her arms rose elegantly above her head, her leg extending out in a graceful point. Each motion was mirrored by the children onstage, in a more remedial form.

Like she'd always been, she was magic.

Something happened to her when she danced, he'd always said. The shy girl that hid in the back of the class became something else. It was how he'd first noticed her in a school talent show. Back then she'd been young, thin as a rail, but strong and lean. Dancing put a power in her that wasn't noticeable when she walked down the hall.

Looking at her now she seemed softer somehow. The hard strength quieter and even more elegant than he remembered.

"So does absence make the heart grow fonder again?" Mary giggled next to him.

Damn. He'd forgotten she was there. With a purse of his lips he shook his head. "No. I always thought she was gorgeous when she danced. It's just been a long time since I've seen it."

"Sure. Whatever you say, Alan."

He waved her off and moved toward the stage. A few more greetings hit his ears as he moved to the nearby food truck. Now unable to see her, he ordered his coffee and stepped back out of the way to let others order. Secretly he was glad for the respite of seeing Ivy dance more. Mary hadn't been too far off the mark. Just seeing her move in subtle movements off the side of a stage had reawakened feelings he'd thought long gone.

The crowd began to clap, and he politely tapped his college ring against the metal casing of the food truck. All the girls rushed to the side of the stage and tugged Ivy from just backstage onto the flimsy platform. A pleasing pink flush filled her cheeks as it always did when she received applause. She gave a simple curtsy, but the girls would not let her go so easily.

A young girl with dark chestnut hair ran to the edge of the stage and hit a few buttons on the CD player. *The Dance of the Sugarplum Fairy* started almost immediately. Ivy waved her hands and shook her head, but the girls pushed her to the front of the stage and then crowded near the exits to block escape.

Ivy's shoulders heaved in a sigh, but her hands moved to position. Without another moment's hesitation her feet flicked in a complex step. He knew the moment her eyes closed she had let the music take over. A deep breath filled his lungs and his heart picked up its cadence when she started to move.

Once, a long time ago, his analytical mind had struggled to make sense of her moves and memorize them, but tonight he just reveled in the motion. Like no time had passed since he'd last seen her in the ballet, she leapt and turned, balancing effortlessly en pointe before falling back into another turn.

Every pause was like a breath, every step a beat of his heart. It wasn't until she stopped along with the music that he even remembered to breathe again. This time he joined more enthusiastically in the applause, clanging his ring against the food truck a little harder. He held off from whistling as her students crowded around her and they all took their bows again together.

He drank down his now lukewarm coffee and tossed it into the trash. It would be foolish to go over and see her now. They'd parted terms as good friends, but then lost touch. He never expected to feel anything akin to what she'd re-sparked in him with just one dance. In just a few weeks he'd be going back to the city and never see her again. It was best to leave that door closed.

"Didn't you see? Well of course you didn't, you were with the little ones. Now, where did he go? Oh there he is! Alan!" He turned at the sound of the voice and saw Mary walking briskly toward him. The meddling gossip she always was, couldn't just let this go, could she? "Look, you walked right on past the stage. Ivy's right here." He was helpless to stop Mary as she marched toward him, with none other than Ivy in tow.

"Alan? My God, it is you!" Ivy's bright laugh, which he recognized now as the one that haunted his dreams, trilled through the air. "How are you?"

He accepted her embrace. With a sigh, he realized he had been right. She was softer now. The harsh, strict lines of her prima days had softened. From what he could tell from the hug, they'd softened in all the right places. Gentle curves accented the toned lines of her arms and back. "Ivy. I had no idea you were back in Lake Point."

"Been here for almost eight years," she whispered in his ear. "I'm sorry I didn't say goodbye."

"You did. You just didn't say you would come back here."

When she pulled back he could've sworn he saw the glimmer of a tear at the edge of her emerald eyes. With a blink it was gone and she smiled. "No. I didn't tell you that part, did I? Goodness, you look good. How have you been?"

"Busy," he replied, chuckling when she said it at the same time as he did. "So the same as always, I guess."

"I guess." Her soft smile brought gentle lines around her lips and eyes, dimples appearing in her cheeks where she'd once been too thin to see them.

"Time has treated you well. You look good."

Her smile twitched and she nodded. Experience told him she was holding back a large laugh. "Thank you. It hasn't been too shabby on you, either."

"That's it?" Mary huffed. "My goodness. You two haven't seen each other in how long…Ivy, didn't you tell me you two were married? Aren't you going to let him see—"

"Mary Denise Powell. I know your mother didn't teach you to be so nosy." Stern lines creased Ivy's brow, reminding him of the danger of facing her wrath. Ivy had always had a temper on her. "I think Alan and I can manage to have an adult conversation, despite not having seen each other in a few years. We have been able to communicate for most of our lives together and apart."

"Apart?" Damn, the appearance of the line had made Mary even nosier. The woman's nostrils flared as her eyebrows shot up behind her bangs. "Wait, but I thought…"

"Do you really want to go there?" Ivy sighed. "Just go congratulate your daughter for a job well done tonight. I'll see you at the tree lighting."

Before Mary could even think to argue, Ivy grabbed his forearm and dragged him away from their former classmate. The music faded now that it was aimed in the opposite direction and for a few minutes nothing but the soft *clop* of her pointe shoes breached the quiet between them.

She stopped at the edge of one of the buildings lining the square and leaned on the railing over the stairs leading to the lower level. A soft smirk graced her lips. "Having to be friends with her now as an adult makes me appreciate being such a loser in high school. I didn't have to deal with her and her gossipy self."

Alan let out a loud laugh. "I did always hate that."

"Welcome home, Alan."

"It's not home."

Her brows pinched together and she looked off down the empty street. "No. I suppose it isn't."

* * * *

Ivy let out a long breath in the silence that lingered between them. The last thing she'd expected was for him to actually return to Lake Point just because his dad was sick. Even if Alan's dad, Sean, was on his deathbed, Ivy knew that Alan found his father's transgressions unforgivable. Out of habit she pressed the tip of her toe into the ground and stretched out her foot before switching to the left.

"Nervous?" A quiet smirk teased the corner of his lips. The same gorgeous chocolate eyes gleamed in a familiar hint of mischief. Time had wrinkled the corners of his eyes, and grayed his chestnut hair at the temples, but he still could take her breath away with one well-placed smile if he wanted to.

"No. Why would you ask that?" She stopped stretching her feet and folded her arms across her chest. Maybe she was being defensive, but he'd caught her off-guard, and there were so many things he didn't know. She didn't even know where to begin.

"You always do that with your feet when you're nervous. Used to do it before every audition. I remember standing in those sweat-stinky halls waiting along with you."

The smile formed before she could stop it, and she laughed. "Like you minded watching dozens of young nubile women bending in ways considered indecent in normal society all in the name of stretching."

"Well, being your support system did have its perks." And there it was. The once 100-watt smile had now grown to a blazing 1,000-watts. Probably had work done to his teeth to keep them perfect, she thought ruefully.

She tried to fight the small melt of her heart and shrugged. "I did try to make sure you had plenty of perks...when we were dating and when we were friends."

"Dating?"

"Fine." She offered a labored huff of a sigh. "Living together. Whatever."

This time his laughter joined hers, but it faded quickly enough. "I didn't expect to find you here. What are you doing back in Lake Point? Your career was still going strong, you were dating that dancer last time we..."

The hesitation in his tone made her giggle. "What? Hooked up? You want me to brag that we lived together but you're embarrassed that we hooked up for one last fling while I was dating another man?"

His nose wrinkled. "Hooked up sounds awful crass."

"It is, and so is what we did that night." She grinned and leaned back against the railing. "Nothing to be ashamed of. I told Justin about it, and he understood."

"You told him?" His eyes couldn't have gotten rounder.

"Of course. I wasn't ashamed. Justin and I suffered no delusions about our relationship. It was fine. It's not like anyone that lives in that world is naïve about relationships. There was quite a bit of hopping with those not being exclusive."

"Huh." His chin jutted out and he folded his arms across his chest. "The things you learn."

"You would be shocked at some of the things I never told you." The teasing note of the conversation was nice and easy. She didn't want to change it. All it would take is distraction and getting him back to his mother. They didn't need to talk about anything deeper. He'd be going back soon enough and life would be quiet again. Well, as quiet as it could be. As quiet as it had been for seven years.

"All stories I would like to hear one day."

"Of course you would."

He leaned on the railing next to her. "You look good, Ivy. Real good."

"I'm in good lighting—candlelight and moonlight are the best. Just don't come to the studio— fluorescent lighting is a beast."

A soft chuckle floated through the air and he shook his head. "I doubt it will make one bit of difference."

"You'd be surprised." She kept her tone droll. "I'd like to see you under it, maybe then I could see the plastic surgery scars."

"Har har har." He gave her shoulder a gentle nudge. After a few minutes he sighed and ran his hand through his hair. "Why did Mary think we'd been married and divorced?"

"Because we left together, I came back alone, and she likes a good story." Her answer was too quick, and the way he snapped his head toward her she could tell he knew it. The anticipation of the inevitable question made her too quick to answer.

"Ivy?"

One foot arched up and stretched out. With a slight bounce she switched again. "Alan, it's been eight years. When I left the city I did it without looking back. I didn't want to talk about the life I'd left, and that led to speculation. People guessed. Despite the fact that Mama Dotty told everyone we'd never been married—well, they talked anyway. Thought maybe she was protecting you from looking like the bad guy."

"Why would I need protecting?"

"That's a very long story." She reached up to tug the pins from her bun. The tension fairly radiated off him, although she didn't know why he was so upset. Dotty herself said that every so often she'd try to tell him that Ivy had moved back, and he always refused to talk about her. Ivy supposed she could have called him herself, but she'd been busy in ways he couldn't know or imagine.

"I'm waiting."

"I don't have time right now. It's the Christmas celebration. I've already been gone too long." With one final tug of her rubber band her hair tumbled free and spilled down her back. Before she could divulge further his hand circled her arm and he pulled her close against him.

He sighed and his forehead pressed to hers. "Ivy."

"A minute ago you were ready to yell at me for not talking. Now what?"

"I don't know. I didn't think I missed you. But I do."

The words burned through her heart like a hot poker. Her throat swelled shut and she pressed her hands into his chest. "We don't know each other anymore. We haven't for a long time. It's why we split, remember? Different worlds?"

"But we stayed friends. I never stopped loving you."

"Neither did I. That still doesn't mean we were ever right for each other. I'm sorry I never said goodbye. I just didn't want—"

"Mom. Mom, come here." The familiar voice cut into their conversation. Justina skipped toward them, stopping short when she saw Alan. "Who's that, Mom?"

Alan's grasp on her arms slackened and he almost shoved her away from him. The cool air that replaced his heat paled to the cold stare he set on her after a good look at Justina. Like everyone else in town she could almost see him counting back years and making assumptions.

"Justina. Come here, baby." Ivy waved over the young girl and smoothed her hand over the chestnut hair when she drew close. Justina pressed into her side and Ivy looked up at Alan. "This is Justina, my daughter. Justina, this is an old friend of mine. It's Miss Dotty's son. You've seen his picture at her house."

"Hello." Justina's voice was small and timid, her greeting out of required politeness.

"Hello." Alan's jaw set tight. "It's nice to meet you. How old are you?"

"Seven."

That did it. Alan shut down cold as ice, anger clouding the hints of regret he'd carried a few seconds ago.

Ivy sighed and squeezed Justina's shoulder. "I still need to change my shoes. I'll meet you and Uncle Jake at the food truck for hot cocoa, okay?"

Justina nodded and darted away. After three steps she paused long enough to mutter a polite goodbye before she disappeared back toward the celebration.

"I should go change." Ivy ran her fingers though her hair and moved to step around him.

"So you let me be the bad guy all these years when I didn't even know?" He stepped into her path with a frown. "Real convenient for you."

"Real presumptuous of you, don't you think?" Even if she understood the assumption, she didn't like to think that he, of all people, would think her capable of such a thing. "You've known me for years and you just assume I would do that?"

"We haven't known each other for years. You just said so yourself."

She bristled and straightened her spine. "Assume whatever you want, you jackass."

"How could you?"

He really thought she'd keep his own child from him? Really? She slapped him hard. "Get your head out of your ass. I'm not a total bitch. How dare you accuse me of keeping a child from you! Did you not hear her name? Justina. As in Justin—the man I was dating last time we saw each other."

"She's seven."

"She isn't yours. Justin and I waited until we could be sure I wasn't pregnant before we ever slept together. He had brown hair too, numbskull. God, I don't remember you being such a hateful bastard. I didn't say it before, but I'll say it now. Goodbye, Alan."

"Ivy."

She shoved off his hand and rushed back to the stage to change. Part of her worried that he'd follow her. Another part of her worried that he wouldn't.

Damn it.

Tears burned her eyes as she dropped down next to her bag and buried her face in her hands. Of all the people to think she'd keep a child from Alan, for it to be Alan himself. The man that once knew her better than anyone.

She expected everyone else to make assumptions. But Alan?

Maybe she was right. Maybe she hadn't known him at all.

Chapter Two

Ivy stretched her legs to either side of her until she felt the familiar pull on muscle. She twirled her toes in circles and closed her eyes. The past couple of days she'd found herself much more tense and snappy than usual. Even Justina had noticed.

It wouldn't do her any good to carry the attitude into classes this afternoon. She was determined to work out every bit of it before students began to arrive after school let out.

Sitting on the ground, with a deep breath, she raised her arms above her head and pointed her toes to the floor. On the exhale she lowered her body until her head touched the ground, the last bit of her exhale released into the floor.

Inch by inch she crept her fingers forward until she could rest her chin on the floor, at which point she flexed her feet. The tension of the stretch pulled out the kinks that had begun to form.

Somehow, with one long overdue visit to his family, Alan had managed to disrupt her sense of calm and order. Years ago they'd parted on amicable terms.

She knew she'd always love him, but their dreams were so disparate.

The opposite natures that had attracted them to each other had made their lives too dissimilar. When they were together they rarely saw each other, even living under the same roof. Breaking up just made sense then. Their careers had always come first, the driving need to succeed, until they realized where they'd ended up.

Still, he'd continued to come to opening and closing night of every show. To take her out to celebrate new roles, or his own accomplishments in big finance, of which there'd been so many. Inevitably, so often, they'd ended up in each other's arms again at the end of the evening. It was familiar and comfortable, but in the morning they returned to their lives, the promises to call faded.

Since the last time she'd seen him, the last thing she'd meant to do was end up in bed with him again. In fact, it was the exact *opposite* of what she was supposed to be doing. It had almost ruined everything she had worked for since she'd left.

Tears burned her eyes again and she wiped at them with a sniffle. She straightened and pulled her legs in front of her.

So much for relieving that tension. Inexorably, her mind went back where it shouldn't. The bells on her door jingled and she hopped to her feet on instinct. She wiped at a lingering tear and walked over to peek in the front room. The waiting area should have been empty at this time, but instead the man of her current consternation stood there in his well-cut jacket.

"Ivy." He tilted his head at her. So formal. Apparently Dotty had forced his hand in this one.

Well, Dotty wasn't here to force Ivy's hand. She tightened her lips and spun on her heel back into the studio. *It would be childish to blast the stereo. You aren't childish, Ivy. Don't be childish.*

"Mom tells me your parents are in Florida now."

"Yup." Silence fell. She didn't bother to initiate as she faced the bar and began basic exercises in an attempt to ignore him.

He cleared his throat. "Mom says I should listen."

"She also says you should talk to your father. Don't see that happening any time soon, either." *Tendu, fifth, dèveloppé, hold.* Teeth clenched together, she tried to focus, but her leg quivered for a moment. With a sigh, she dropped it. "Justina is most certainly not your daughter. What else is there to say?"

"I don't get any explanation? You do let people believe she's mine, after all."

"I do *not*." She spun and charged across the room right up in his face. "I have told everyone several times that you and I were never married. After all, it wasn't within our career goal guidelines. I've told them Justin is her father. They just assume I'm trying to make you look better because you are the one so driven you stayed in New York."

"And you let them."

A laugh escaped and she threw up her hands. "Aren't you listening? I'm sorry that I don't correct every single reference. That I don't put it on a billboard. You and I were in love when we left Lake Point. We stayed together for years. People assume no matter what I or your mother tell them. It happens. Get over yourself."

"And where is Justin? Why isn't he defending himself?" Alan folded his arms across his chest.

The venom faded at the mention of Justin. She backed off and turned away. Angry as she was at him, she wasn't about to let him see the grief she still carried. "He's gone."

"Convenient."

She straightened her back. "No. It really isn't."

"Of course it is. For him."

"He's dead, you asshole. Get out of my studio."

"Ivy." Now he bothered to sound worried, kind, caring. The very parts of him that had made her cling to him so long despite his ruthless business nature. "I didn't know."

"Now you do. Get out of my studio."

* * * *

"The nerve of that asshole." Ivy paced the small office.

Behind the desk her friend Eve didn't bother to stop grinning. Eve was a beautiful blond with a body Ivy would kill for with its curves, but Eve was too self-conscious and self-deprecating to ever agree. If she did, maybe she'd actually hook up with her boss and best friend, Jake. "You are so in love."

"I was. Now I'm pissed."

"Fine line, so they say." Eve gathered her purse and rose. "Explain to me again why you never told him about Justina or Justin?"

"He knew I was sort of dating Justin. I never told him what we were really doing or planning, though. You should have seen him." Ivy sighed and leaned against the door frame while Eve donned her coat. "He'd received another promotion, he was only a few steps away from partner and so proud of himself for achieving a goal two years ahead of time."

"Him and his damn spreadsheets and plans." Eve snorted and flipped her long waves out from under her coat. "I swear he had your life planned down to the second when you both took off out of town without ever looking back."

A familiar twinge hit her heart and Ivy shook her head. "No. Not quite that exact then. We both had goals, but his plans were looser and allowed for extraneous details."

"Like marriage?"

"I thought. Maybe. Once." Ivy pushed open the door and welcomed the shock of cold air that froze any burning hint of rising tears. "Where to?"

"You need a junk food binge with all of this drama. Where do you think?"

"The Midway." Ivy grinned and laced her arm through Eve's. "You're right. I rarely indulge, but it sounds perfect. Just tell me you have the antacids."

"I never leave home without them." Eve chuckled. "So what are you going to do?"

"Same thing I always do. Alan won't stick around long, he'll take his first excuse and head out of here like a rocket back to the city. Then life can return to normal."

"Life hasn't been normal since you left the city." Eve held up her hands in defense when Ivy spun on her. "It's been good, but it hasn't been normal."

The words stung more than Ivy cared to admit, because that would mean they were true. She'd never been in love with Justin, and he hadn't been in love with her. They cared for each other, but they'd also both left their hearts with another. They'd both known it when they'd gone down the path they'd chosen. That was it, though, it was their choice. She'd always loved Alan, but he succeeded much further with his goals when she wasn't in his way.

Eve pushed open the door to The Midway and the bright yellow walls and the ping of the skeeball machine interrupted the morose tone that had descended on the conversation. Instantly Ivy brightened up. Eve was grinning right along with her. "Can't help but be happy in this place. Hey Mikey!"

Michaela O'Keefe, the stereotypically red-haired owner of the fair-themed restaurant smiled at them both. "Eve, Ivy. It's great to see you in here. Normally you never come without Justina tagging along."

"I'm the one dragging her along. She needed the junk food far more than I do." Eve patted her ass before she leaned in. "Alan's back."

"He's not back," Ivy protested. "Not really. He's just visiting."

Mikey went slack-jawed for a moment before she recovered. "Oh dear. Let me guess, Philly steak, no peppers?"

"Please. And a huge order of fries." Ivy nodded. "I need them today."

"Same for me, but I'll take the peppers she doesn't want." Eve frowned. "I'd ask you to join us, but you look swamped and stressed. Why don't you hire an assistant manager already?"

"I haven't even had time to place the ad. I've asked some of my older employees, but they all want to stay part time. I don't have time to search." Michaela rang them up and called back their order before she sighed. "Once the holiday rush is over I'll place an ad."

"You need someone now. When was your last day off?" Ivy glanced around the packed restaurant. "You're only closed on the holidays."

"I was just off on Thanksgiving. I'm fine, really." Michaela handed them a balloon with their order number on it. "I like keeping busy. It's better than the alternative."

Ivy took the balloon and followed Eve to a table where she dropped the weighted sack holding the balloon down onto the floor. Once she sat, the balloon bobbed above their heads. She pulled out a few napkins and laid them across her lap, and then leaned on the table.

"She does kind of look like him, you know." Eve slurped her water up through her straw, one eyebrow curved up like she dared Ivy to object. "If someone didn't know better and looked for him, they'd see him in her."

"I know." Ivy's shoulders dropped as she released the tension. "The fate of genetics gave her enough of Justin that she would favor Alan. Justin used to tease me that the only reason I gave him a second look was because of his similarity to Alan."

"Didn't you guys used to double date with Justin and…"

"Julie. Yes." Ivy pulsed her straw through her water. "Until Julie went to San Francisco. Alan and I were still on again, off again, at that point. Alan and Justin used to try to tell people they were fraternal twins."

"Then you could call it an honest mistake."

"An honest mistake which managed to accuse me of being a horrible bitch that would keep a child from Alan." Ivy shoved her glass away and sank down in her chair. While Eve was one of the few people that knew, and believed, the whole story, she still didn't know everything. "I made a choice, but if it had been his child I never would have kept it from him. Justina could have been his. I was so full of hormones, we are very lucky the condom was sound."

Eve giggled when a few heads turned their way. "You said that a little loud."

"Oops." Ivy laughed, relaxing more as Eve lost control of her laughter. Soon enough Ivy joined in and by the time the food arrived she'd happily changed the subject.

* * * *

Alan's leg bobbed under the table at a furious pace. The hem of the napkin folded and twirled in the pinch and turn of his fingers.

Dotty punched him hard in the thigh. "Knock it off."

"Sorry, Mom." He clenched his jaw. "Why didn't you just tell me?"

"Why did you assume Ivy would keep a child from you? I never once thought she'd keep my grandchild from me, although I'm grateful she lets me play that role in Justina's life. I think it helps us all." She pursed her lips. "Even more than that, why did you assume I wouldn't tell you?"

He winced and jerked his finger toward the office where his dad lay with his hospice nurse nearby. "I never let you talk about anything much. I always think you're going to bring *him* up." The heartburn that had plagued him for days flared up his esophagus and threatened to burn a hole through his throat. Stress he was used to, stress he could handle. All of this was new. It had been years since he'd bothered with emotions. Since Ivy.

"Something like this I would have told you. Period." She sighed and set her knitting in her lap. "I don't even know what happened. Ivy's never told me. All we knew was that she came back home quite pregnant, and it wasn't yours. She's a good mom. I think being back here has done her good. Might do you good, too."

He scratched his neck, the uncomfortable thought of all the quiet made him twitch. "I sincerely doubt it."

The doorbell pealed through the house. One of his mom's miniature schnauzers in the back room started to bark.

"That would be them. Why don't you go check on the dogs while I prepare Ivy for your presence?"

He grunted and pushed himself to his feet. "She's going to be mad you lied to her."

"Please. I'm sure she already knows." His mom patted her silver, curly hair like there might be a lock out of place. "It's only because of Justina wanting to see the puppies all the time that led her to agree to have coffee with me this afternoon. Now go on, check the pups. I'll make sure Ivy is settled down before you see her."

Still grumbling, he went back to the small guest bedroom. He had to hold a foot out to stop Chester, the oldest schnauzer from getting out. When the pup moved to leap over to greet the guests, Alan snatched him out of the air and held him up to his chest. "Fast little mongrel, aren't you. Old as you are, you should be slow and decrepit."

He shut the door to the sound of Ivy's voice mixing with his mom's and set Chester back down in the empty pen. The small whimpers and yips from the corner drew him closer, and he grinned down at the pile of puppies eagerly going for their food. Soon enough they'd be fully weaned and ready to be given to the new owners.

It was a *hobby* his mom said. One she'd picked up when he left town, coincidentally. Breeding miniature schnauzers hadn't been his first pick for her, but it kept her busy. Right then it was probably the only reason she didn't spend every waking minute in his father's hospice room. Having pups to take care of gave her something other than his dad to worry about, thank God.

Footsteps pounded down the hall and Chester started going mad again moments before the door burst open. The huge grin on Justina's features dissolved into wide green eyes. There was a nervous flutter to her hand when she tucked a lock of hair behind her ear, just like her mother.

"Sorry. Didn't mean to startle you." Alan smiled and waved her in. "I'm guessing you're here to see the puppies. Don't let me stop you, I'm just checking on them."

"Okay." She didn't need to be told twice, although her steps were still a little shy. Once she was at the edge of the pen, a happy sigh escaped. "Mama says maybe the next litter I can have one."

Alan paused partway to the door, startled she spoke to him. He swallowed against the uncomfortable lump in his throat. Children weren't something he was accustomed to dealing with in his daily life. He didn't have anything against them, they just didn't fit in his life.

"I asked Santa for one, though."

That brought a smile to his face and he walked back over. He dropped down to crouch next to the pen. "You asked Santa, did you? By letter?"

She cast him a sideways glance that gave him the impression she thought he was completely insane. "Letter? No. Email, of course."

"Of course, how silly of me. Santa would have email now, wouldn't he?" He chuckled and shook his head. "It's been a long time since I've talked to Santa. When I did we used letters."

"You must be *old*."

He snorted. "I am. I'm pretty damn old."

"You shouldn't say damn." She shrugged at his continued laughter. "Mama says it's a bad word."

"Well, it certainly isn't a nice word." Alan nodded. "So I'm sorry."

"It's okay. Mama says it too when she thinks I can't hear." She sighed. "I really wanted that one."

Alan grinned when he realized she pointed at the runt of the litter. "She's awful small. You sure you'd want a puppy that's the littlest?"

"She's different. Like me."

"You don't look too different to me." He tilted his head and narrowed his eyes. In the daylight he realized what a fool he had been. Despite her hair color, she looked nothing like him. Ivy's eyes and nose, the rest was clearly Justin. He remembered Justin well. "I mean, I don't see any extra eyes. Unless, you don't have one hiding in the back of your head do you?"

She giggled at his dramatic gasp and attempt at a horrified expression. With her lips pinched tight between her teeth she shook her head fast.

He leaned in closer to whisper. "Extra toes?"

"Ewww." Nose wrinkled, she turned a little green. "Feet are nasty."

"Ah, that's right. You've been around your mom's feet. I see why you think that. Dancers have some messed up feet."

"I'm a dancer." She straightened, her chin lifted. Every haughty inch of her mirroring Ivy's proud stance.

"But without pointe shoes, so I'm sure your feet are still perfectly lovely." He tipped his head with a heaping of chagrin. "So please accept my apologies for the rather uncalled for insinuation."

"You're funny."

He chuckled. "I thank you for thinking so."

"Alan." His mom leaned on the door frame, a gentle smile on her features. "Son, why don't you go have some coffee? I'm going to let Justina play with our little runt for a while."

"Sure thing Mom. Lady Justina." Alan rose to full height before bowing. "I'll see you soon."

"Okey dokey. Miss Dotty, come look. Her brother's pushing her out of the way again. It's not fair."

He accepted his mom's hug on the way past. "Should I be ready for war?"

"You should be ready to make it right." She smacked his arm and moved over to Justina's side.

Alan stopped in the middle of the hallway and adjusted his tie. For the past eight years, without the distraction of Ivy, his life had gone exactly according to the plan he'd always had. He hadn't realized what a distraction she'd been.

Now he was starting to realize how much he missed that distraction. How much he'd missed her. At one time, when she'd first disappeared, he'd planned to try to find her. It was always at the top of the list, but it was a list he never got around to.

Of course he'd dated plenty since she'd left, they both had. At least, he'd assumed she had. And perhaps still did.

How was it that just seeing her again got him confused? The choice they'd made to permanently split up had been logical for them both. It also got them both right where they wanted to be. He thought that as his career moved forward, that maybe she'd disappeared from New York to go on to San Francisco or maybe even overseas like she'd dreamed.

Not back here to Lake Point, teaching children with little hope of reaching the heights she'd reached. Never that.

With another deep breath he headed down the hall to the kitchen. Sunlight streamed into the dim hall. The kitchen had two walls filled with windows, lending a ton of light in the back of the house to contradict the dark and narrow hallways everywhere else.

In the corner sat the table with bench seating lining the walls. Ivy perched on a seat, feet up and arms on her knees. The coffee cup in her hand steamed, the scent of sweet vanilla reaching his nose. She still drank her coffee the same way.

He grabbed the coffee pot and poured himself a cup. "I'm sorry."

She slurped her drink in place of an answer.

"Mature."

All he got for that one was a shrug.

He sighed and walked over. Without an invitation he sat on the bench near her feet. "I don't have an explanation. Not one that would satisfy your anger. It just caught me off-guard seeing her."

Her lips thinned, but then she sighed. "Seeing you again caught me off-guard."

"The feeling's mutual." He wanted to touch her, his fingers twitched in their attempt to rest on her foot. "Am I forgiven?"

"You accused me of keeping a secret child from you. Of leaving town without a word and having the baby and never, ever telling you."

"So I owe you dinner?"

Despite what appeared to be a strong attempt to stop it, her lips twitched. "I'm a single mother. I can't just skip out for dinner whenever I want."

"I'm sure Mom would watch her for three days if that's how long it took you and I to talk this out. I bet if we asked nice, she'd watch Justina for dinner."

"That's true," she hedged. "I suppose dinner would be fine."

This time he didn't resist the urge, and set his hand on her foot. "Once you and I have had a chance to talk, I'll take both of you out."

She took another loud slurp of coffee. At his snort, she grinned into her coffee. "It might take more than dinner."

"I can handle more than dinner."

"I didn't mean that, Alan."

"Too bad. I did."

She blushed a deep pink, and looked back out the window. "I know."

Chapter Three

Alan parked in the driveway of a modest brick ranch-style house. The house was set back in a private cul-de-sac off the main road, on a road lined with trees now bare in the grasp of a cold winter. The lawns weren't, though, and a vibrant snowball war raged on several houses away.

Once he'd shut off the rental car and stepped out, he felt a nervous clutch of his stomach. It seemed silly to be nervous about dinner with Ivy of all people.

Still, she was so different. Time had softened some edges and hardened others. He worried about stepping into a mine field by saying the wrong thing.

By the time he rang the bell, a chuckle had started to rise. He became painfully aware of the fact that he felt right now the same way he had on their first date back when they'd been fifteen. She'd been quite an enigma to him then, too.

The laugh that had been forming choked up in his throat the moment the door opened. He coughed several times to try to rid himself of the sensation and held up a finger in her bewildered face. Several coughs later he felt in control enough to straighten, although the reflex still had him jerking. "Sorry."

Amusement tugged at her red lips. "No problem." She'd gone all out. Most likely she'd guessed he planned to take her to a nice place. Her dress was purple and black and hugged her new-found curves just right.

Under the dress her legs were swathed in tights that had intricate lacy patterns all over them, revealing peeks at her legs. Her feet were still shoe-less, leaving her arching them in anxious anticipation.

He made no effort to rush, despite the wide open door in the middle of winter. Each inch was covered again, up her legs, hips, waist, breasts that hadn't been quite that luscious before.

She'd left her hair partially down and long waves of auburn swept down over her shoulder to her waist. As always, off-stage her makeup was impeccable and drew every bit of his attention to her emerald green eyes.

One eyebrow quirked and she teased him with another smile. "It's nothing you haven't seen before."

"Those are new." He purposely looked back at her chest. "Motherhood did you good in many ways, Ivy."

"Pig."

"Oink."

She giggled, a wonderful carefree and musical sound. "Get your ass inside before I freeze mine off."

It lightened his heart that they were starting off the night on a good enough note. He knew his mom had picked up Justina hours ago. Something about plans for the bounce house, whatever that was. The time really had been well-used by Ivy. She looked like a million bucks. "You look amazing."

"You have nostalgic goggles on, but I appreciate the sentiment." She gathered her cell phone and keys into a small purse. "Did I guess correctly about dinner? I was worried I'd be dressed inappropriately. What you're wearing is no indication, you'd be wearing that same thing if we were the ones going to the bounce house."

"Ouch." He clutched his chest in a dramatic gesture. "The lady doth wound me."

"The man still be a pig."

"You're dressed perfect. I'm taking you to Epoque."

She paused with her finger hooked on the heel she was putting on. "Epoque? We're going into Rochester?"

"Of course. Did you expect me to take you to Antonio's because it's the nicest place in town? Just because they serve Italian and keep the place dim doesn't mean it's fancy or romantic." He chuckled.

"I don't know if I can handle Epoque. It's been a long time since I ate food that rich. I don't exercise like I did then." Now that she had her heels on, she almost met him eye to eye.

He grabbed the coat she had on a chair near the door and held it out for her. "One night of decadence isn't going to do anything but spoil you for goulash."

"I have never made goulash, thank you." She was still chuckling when she took his hand. "But it might spoil me to my favorite sandwich."

"I'm afraid to ask what it is."

"Oh, I'm not going to spoil the surprise. I fully intend to make you one. You'll never want to eat anything else again."

"When do I get this treat of a sandwich?"

A sly smile curved her lips and she paused halfway into the car. One long leg in, one long leg out, she straightened until they were eye to eye. "Depends."

"On?"

"How tonight goes."

* * * *

The layout of the restaurant afforded an elegant lounge to begin or end the night in, or even eat off a lesser menu. Ivy was glad Alan chose to take advantage of the lounge to start their night with cocktails and an appetizer.

Then again, she couldn't imagine he could be hungry with the way he'd devoured her with his eyes back at the house. Once again, she felt a smile starting to build at the memory. The fact that he'd noticed the way her body had filled out, meager as some assets were, pleased her to no end.

Not that it should. Alan had no intent on staying around Lake Point any longer than necessary. As always and forever, it seemed, their goals were once again taking them in such different directions.

This time she had a daughter to think about. A daughter that didn't need to get curious about the oddity of a man in her mother's world after the utter absence of one. Ivy would not play with her daughter's heart like that, especially when it was a sure bet Alan would leave town at his earliest opportunity. Alan's offer to take them both out had to be off the table and remain there.

Then again, it had been so long since she had been able to enjoy the company of a man, she couldn't imagine turning down this opportunity. As long as she kept Alan to herself for a little while, it wouldn't hurt anything. She could handle it.

Sure, it might sting to lose him again, but by now she was used to their relationship not working. It hadn't in so long, and he'd been in and out of her life so many times, once more wouldn't hurt.

She hoped.

"Here you are. Best wine on the menu." Alan returned to their table with their glasses and slid into the comfortable seat beside her. His own glass was filled with the rich amber color of what was likely the best scotch within the state. "I ordered some calamari.

Now we can relax until we're ready to go to the table."

"Thank you." She held the glass in her lap by its base. If the evening were to have any hope of ending well, they had to get the unpleasant parts out of the way. "So where would you like to start?"

"You want to do this now? Here?"

"Well, where else?"

"I thought after a nice dinner we'd go back to your place."

She shook her head firmly. "No. This isn't pillow talk. If you want any hope of that ever happening, we do it now." The minute the words left her mouth, she cringed.

"Nice choice of words." He chuckled and set his glass on the table. When hers remained untouched in her lap, he took it and set it on the table as well. "Okay, if we're doing this, then I have to admit I was curious about what you said. That you waited long enough to be sure there wasn't a baby after we were together last."

The touch of his finger to her cheek made her wince, and she took a ragged breath when he brushed a lock of hair behind her ear. She braced her hands on the seat and lifted enough to shift herself to face him. "That's not far enough back. You remember Justin, don't you?"

"I remember several dinners with him. He was in your ballet company. Wasn't he with your friend Julie, the other prima?"

"Yes." She smiled. "I went on a lot of double dates with them. With you, with other men I dated. Justin and I were friends. Good friends."

He drank a sip of scotch, but kept his eyes on her. "What changed?"

"Not much. Well, everything. Julie got a job in San Francisco. They tried for a while to make the long-distance thing work, but of course it didn't. After a year they gave up. It was another year before Justin and I started to get closer."

By now his scotch was forgotten on the table again. As if he sensed her racing heart, the sick twist of her stomach, his hand settled on hers.

"We were just figuring things out. We were talking about a possible future after the ballet. At almost thirty, it was what we talked about. What we'd do after. In many ways I cared for him so deeply, in others…"

Alan's brow furrowed.

"He wasn't you. I wasn't Julie. But you never wanted children. Neither did Julie. Julie was younger by five years. She wasn't seeing the end as close as Justin and I." She pinched her tongue between her teeth hard to get the rising tears under control. A handkerchief appeared before her and she took it from Alan gratefully.

"I never said that. I never said I didn't want kids. " It was a quiet, small protest to her declaration.

"Not in so many words. But even when we were younger, in all your talk of the future ahead of us, there was never a mention of children. Not once. I was fine with it when I was seventeen with a dream I wanted to fulfill. In my late twenties, not so much."

His brows knit together, the expression so familiar she was sure she could guess what he was feeling. Frustration, maybe even a little annoyed that she'd guessed so much about him, that she was likely right.

"Kids don't fit in your plans. But your plans, your goals, they were, and are, much longer lasting than mine. No matter what I would have done, mine had a finite end. Dancing always does. I had the nest egg you helped me start and grow—but nowhere else to go. No other life planned, and you had long stopped coming around regularly to help me make one. I had to do this one thing on my own."

After another long drink of scotch, he leaned back and studied her. "Ever think you might just be settling?"

"Of course. Every day I thought that, and Justin did too." She straightened the hem of her dress. "So we backed off for a while. Let ourselves continue seeing each other, and others. I started to plan to come back here on my own. I didn't want to blow the whole nest egg on an apartment in the city, and I knew I could find a nice home here."

"But you love the city." A smile creased his features. "I remember how excited you were that whole first year, and even beyond."

"I do love the city, but when it came time for my retirement, well, I wanted something quiet for myself. I can always visit the city, that doesn't mean I have to live there." Just talking about the decision brought back the familiar pain she'd felt at making it. Torn between two worlds that she loved equally. "It wasn't an easy choice."

"Were you going to tell me about your plan?"

"I knew you'd talk me out of it. So, not until I'd left. I did have every intention of telling you." She bit her lip. "So I told the director my plans for retirement. I would finish the coming season, and leave mid-show of the last show. I didn't want to go out on a closing night, but in the middle of the run."

"So I wouldn't know it was your final night, because it would be mentioned in the program. I was always at opening and closing night."

"You hadn't been for a long time."

"Yes, I had."

Cold shock numbed her fingers, and she pulled them closer to her for warmth. "Well, I never saw you, did I? So the decision had nothing to do with your presence. My choice was made and I would slip away mid-show."

He leaned forward then, the pad of his thumb brushed a tear from her cheek. "And what about Justin?"

She sniffed and wiped at another tear. "We were still close. At least until he left the company very suddenly. I knew he'd been having pain that he'd been hiding from everyone. He blamed it on an old injury. When he disappeared without an explanation to me I was worried. He wouldn't answer my calls, just stopped talking to me."

"Like me."

"No. Not like you." A smile crept through her sadness. "You and I are both to blame for letting ourselves grow apart. I hold you at no more fault than myself."

"If he disappeared, how did you end up with Justina?"

"Justin showed up on my doorstep about six months before you did. I knew right away something was wrong. He looked terrible. Gaunt." She steepled her hands over her nose and pressed in an attempt to stem the flow of tears. "Cancer, he told me."

A warm hand rested on her shoulder, and then he moved next to her. He held her gently against him. "I'm sorry."

A pitiful laugh escaped. "It's been almost nine years. I should be able to tell this by now." She let out another heavy breath. "If I told you everything, we'd be here for hours longer. Suffice it to say, it was sudden and very fast. In the end, when it came down to it, we decided to have a child together. I was retiring anyway, and we thought he might live long enough to see his child born."

His arm tensed as he held her. "Then I showed up."

"I know we were safe as could be, you used a condom...but I was on fertility meds. I never should have slept with you. It set everything back months. Justin understood, though. He knew what it was like when I was around you. How I felt." Her hand shook when she set it over his. "But it did set back our time table, because we had to make sure that you and I didn't accidentally create a baby."

"Mom said when you arrived you were still pregnant."

"Yes." The story mostly told now, the nerves started to ease. Her shoulders relaxed and she leaned against him. "I was six months along when Justin passed. He lived long enough to learn it would be a girl. He was so happy."

He kissed her temple. "I didn't know you ever wanted kids."

"I don't think I did either. But I was ready, and I've never regretted it."

* * * *

They arrived back at Ivy's just before the snow started to fall. Alan hesitated on her porch as Ivy went in, admiring the way the Christmas lights she strung along the bushes illuminated the first clinging flakes of white.

By the looks of it, the snow would be heavy and wet, perfect for a snowball fight. If he still took part in such things. What was it about being back in Lake Point that made him want to do just that?

With a sigh, he turned and followed Ivy inside the house. Ivy's version of *tossing off* her shoes was to set them straight as a pin on a mat by the door. It was one thing he and Ivy had always had in common, an almost OCD tendency toward neatness.

He toed off his shoes and lined them up next to Ivy's. He shed his coat and hung it on the coat rack and continued to follow her into the living room.

Their OCD had helped in their first tiny apartment, and he had to admire the fact that she could still keep her house neat as a pin with a child around. The living room he could see from the kitchen had obvious signs of being used for play-- books, a play kitchen, and other assorted toys were present. However, they all remained tucked in a corner, each in an apparently assigned place.

"I'll get the wine." Ivy walked past and toward the kitchen. She had to have stopped in her bedroom, because she'd changed. The tights were gone, as was, unfortunately, the skimpy purple dress. Not that he could complain as she wore painted-on leggings with a long sweater that just grazed the bottom of her ass, and clung to her curves just as the dress had.

Alan rolled the rising tension out of his shoulders as his cock sprang to life again. That woman could wake him from a coma if she wanted. It probably didn't help that he was living off a six month dry spell. Work and dealing with all the legal matters of hospice and crap for his bastard father had curbed any attempts at dating.

Rather than keep letting his mind wander in that direction. "Looks like it's going to come down heavy."

"Maybe, but they're only predicting four inches." Ivy's voice was muffled and when he rounded the corner to the kitchen he found the pleasant site of her bent over with her head in a wine cooler.

He tilted his head a bit and took in the long, lean length of leg. The sweater rode up so her still firm ass was displayed prominently. "Predictions by good old Charlie Weather? I saw the old nutter was still on channel twelve. He's as useful and trustworthy as an old sock."

Her sweet, musical laugh filled the kitchen and her ass twitched once before she finally stood. "Good point. Well, you're in luck. I knew I had this hidden where it wouldn't be reached all that easily. Mary's a bit on the drunky side. This one is saved special, as I don't get a chance to buy it but once a year."

The smile he'd been sporting threatened to crack his cheeks when he saw the label. "I haven't had that in a while. Still your favorite?"

"You betcha. Have a seat. Make yourself comfortable." She set the bottle in the wine opener on her counter and reached for glasses as she opened it. "So. It's your turn."

He sat as instructed on one of the bar chairs, glad for the excuse to adjust himself. Ivy was driving him to distraction without trying, although he suspected she knew it. After a minute her words sank in. "Sorry? My turn for what?"

"Well, all we did during dinner is talk about me. Where I've been and what I've done, which frankly isn't very exciting." She poured a glass of wine, pausing in her speech long enough to breathe in the scent. "Mmm. Next time I'm in the city I have got to buy more than one bottle to bring home. Although saving it for special occasions does make it taste better."

"You still go to the city?" He accepted the glass she handed him. After her revelation at dinner, the conversation had revolved around her, but mostly in the superficial sense. He was still trying to figure out how to handle the story of her daughter.

"Of course. Once a year Justina and I go out. We go in June when school is done and stay for a few weeks with Justin's parents. Then they come back here for another few weeks and we rent a cottage on the lake over the border."

"So Justina does get to see them. I wondered."

She nodded over her glass of wine. Before she answered her eyes closed and he could tell she was savoring the sweet wine. When the muscles of her neck moved with her swallow she finally opened her eyes again. "Of course. They spend winters in Florida, so we often go down in the fall to visit my parents and usually there's a few days at the theme parks with all the grandparents."

"So you guys get a lot of traveling in. I'm surprised you go to the city."

"Why? I don't hate it. I think it's important Justina get to see the place that meant so much to me. She's been backstage at the ballet and seen quite a few Broadway shows. I actually think she's leaning more toward theater than..." Her words trailed off and for a moment he imagined he could see her building walls. "But yes. We go to the city and you are changing the subject again."

"I'm just curious."

"What about you?" This time she wouldn't let him skirt around it. "It's been eight years since I saw you last. Dotty has been good enough to let me know you are well, but she is also good enough to not go into details unless I ask."

"Not much to tell. You know what sort of life I lead. Work, work, and then there's more work. I've done really well, I'm in the upper echelon at Graystone Financial." Work was a safer area to talk about. From their conversation at dinner, he guessed she hadn't had much chance to date. She didn't need to hear about his escapades.

"Work I know. That your mother feels she can talk to me about. I want to know about you, Alan." She tilted her wine glass in circles, staring at the wine. Then she fixed an intense gaze on him. "Not your work. I'm assuming by the way you have been undressing me all night and having your way with me in your mind that you're currently single?"

"I'm a man." His laughter bubbled out, even as he tugged at his collar after being caught. "I'd do that anyway."

"No. You'd be far more subtle if you were involved. There were a few times I saw you when you happened to be dating someone. You were far more respectful and reserved with your leers."

"See? You do know me."

She flushed a pleasing pink and poured another glass. "I did once."

"Still do. Not that much has changed."

"Everything has changed."

"I suppose it has." His throat suddenly dry, he drank down his wine without savoring it as Ivy did. "I've had a few attempts at a relationship. I dated Sissy Gray for a while."

She choked on her wine, covering her nose with a wince. After she swallowed and coughed a few times she looked at him sideways. "I'm sorry. Did you say Sissy Gray?"

"Yeah."

"As in the socialite, Sissy Gray?" At his nod, her eyes grew wider. "Doesn't she have that reality show? *Life with Sissy?*"

"Why? Do you watch it?" He had to struggle to hold back his laughter as she put the pieces of the puzzle together in her head.

Her wine forgotten for a moment she leaned on the counter across from him. "No. Should I have been? Were you on it? No. Wait. Mary watches it, she would have told me. Were you?"

"No." He chuckled and leaned his forearms on the counter. "I dated her before that circus started. Even if I was still dating her, I wouldn't do a reality show. Those things are atrocious. I don't want to be a part of the media craze."

"So you wouldn't want a wife on the *Real NYC Wives* show, either?"

"God, no." He snorted and leaned back. "Not at all. I barely watch TV. I hardly want to be on it."

"Good to know." She chuckled and picked her wine back up. She took a long, slow sip with her green eyes still focused on him. "Any other celebrities of any list, A-to-D, that I should know about?"

"No. You already knew about Candace." Candace MacAfee had been the longest relationship he'd had with Ivy still in his circle, and since, really. Even Candace had eventually moved on, telling him she wouldn't be with someone in love with another woman. He'd thought she was full of it. But she wasn't the only one to say it.

"I remember. She was a sweetheart. What happened to her?"

"According to her last email, she's happily married and far away from the spotlight. Living in London now." He smiled. "I got to go to the wedding. It was a simple affair in England. Think she met him on set and decided to retire to be with him once the movie was over. Seems pretty happy."

"Good for her. I knew she was too good for all that celebrity crap."

He wondered how long he should let her drag out the small talk. All he wanted to do was touch her again. It had been way too long. From the minute he'd seen her on that stage last week he'd wondered at how she could still make him burn for her like this.

"Promise me you aren't seeing anyone."

The words drew him out of his lust-induced haze and he blinked to clear the last of it away. He furrowed his brow. "I promise. Why?"

"Because the way you were just looking at me, I wasn't sure how long I'd have to think clearly." The red lipstick she wore clung to her lips, making the smile she offered that much more appealing. "And before I lose you again…"

He'd already stood to move closer. When she took a few steps back, he moved forward. Until they were close enough to touch. Just two fingers on each of her hips was enough to make her breath hitch.

She backed into the counter and gripped the edges tight. "Alan."

"Yes?" He'd always loved that even in bare feet she was tall enough he didn't have to bend far to capture her lips. They were already so close. The conversation could wait.

"I'm serious. Please. I have one condition."

"Okay." The tone of her voice made him stop. Stern and strict. He knew better than to mess with her in that mood. He set his hands on the counter on either side of her waist and straightened them so he was back far enough to meet her gaze. "What's the condition?"

"I've known you forever. You've been a part of me for so many years. I'm used to our relationship and what it is. What it's had to be for us to get where we did, and do what we have. I've become as accustomed to seeing your back as you leave, as you are accustomed to seeing mine."

Pain once again lodged a hard hit to his heart, and his throat closed up. Every single time he'd hated leaving. Hated that they both agreed it was logical. It had always been logical and right and gotten them far. But right or not, it still hurt. He could see she was waiting for a response, so he offered a curt nod.

"But I won't let it happen to my daughter. I won't let her get used to you being here for the few weeks you are, only to watch you walk away. Your offer to take her with us on a date is kind, and very accepting of you. But it won't happen."

He tensed. "You don't think I'm good enough to know your daughter?"

"No. That's not it. You can get to know her as you have been. In a group setting where she knows you as Dotty's handsome son that lives far away. Not as a man in my life." She set her hands on his chest. "You are a very good man and if I thought for a second you'd leave the city and move back here I'd allow it. But we both know it would take more than me to make you do that."

He didn't know if he should ignore the level of pain in her voice on her last statement. It matched the way his heart twisted until he was sure he felt it bleeding. Was that really what she thought it came down to? Was it what it came down to? The thought of leaving the city never occurred to him until that moment.

"Alan. Will you do as I ask?"

Words stuck in his throat, his own confusion and pain blurring his answer. "I should go. This is more complicated than it used to be."

"It doesn't have to be. It can be what it's always been." Before he could protest, her soft lips claimed his. She nibbled on his lip as her arms slid up around his neck.

He gripped her waist and helped her jump onto the counter. The gentle tease of her lips became insistent and drove heat right through him. His body didn't need any further convincing, even if his head spun.

Within minutes she helped him forget in the fire of her kiss as her legs wrapped around his waist and pulled him tight against her heat. He moaned when her lips left his to travel down his throat. The tight knot of his tie shifted against his throat before she pulled it loose. "Bedroom?"

"End of hall." She lifted the tie over his head.

"Don't throw away that tie." He brushed his lips across hers and grinned as she let it dangle to the side. "I might want to use it."

She practically purred in her giggle. When he lifted her off the counter she squealed and clung to him all the way down to the end of the hall until the door slammed shut.

Chapter Four

The first thing Ivy noticed when she started to wake was that she was cold. While she'd spent all night wrapped in the warmth of Alan, she was now quite certainly alone.

Next she noticed the inexplicably deep sense of loss his absence now left her with. In spite of her assurances to Alan and herself, perhaps her heart wasn't as able to handle him leaving as it once had. The final separation eight years ago had been the worst. While she'd had the distraction and comfort of Justin, she'd found herself looking over her shoulder constantly in hopes Alan would show up.

Then she'd left the city and focused on her daughter, and the pain had lessened enough that she now was able to lead a full life. Maybe part of her had hoped that one day he'd return, but that was the foolish dreamer she'd once been. The part she couldn't ever seem to shake. The part that kept hoping just once they'd be enough for each other.

She exhaled slowly to release the tension growing in her shoulders and rolled over. By the window Alan sat in her chair, a neglected cup of coffee on the table, his chin perched on his hand as it always was when he got lost in thought. He didn't look toward the bed, but out the window at the snow drifts that led to the park near the lake.

For a minute she let herself enjoy the view. The lines of his nose and mouth silhouetted against the window inexplicably excited her again. It took some effort to not say anything to call him back to bed, at least until her eyes adjusted to the sunlight and she was able to see his expression more clearly.

Trouble lines creased his brow, his lips. She wondered what had him so upset, or if he was feeling the same as she did this morning. Then again, that might be wishful thinking. Maybe he was just planning his exit strategy to get back to the city sooner than planned. He was probably running out of excuses to not see his dad.

Wondering about it felt incredibly stupid. They'd always been able to talk, and there was no point in being afraid to talk now. "Penny for your thoughts."

He started and rubbed his hand over his face. A slow smile curved across his lips. "My thoughts cost way more than a penny these days."

"Did I lose my discounted rate, then?"

"Never." He sighed and twirled the coffee mug on the side table. "Guess telling you I was thinking about work won't cut it?"

"Nope. That wasn't your 'work thoughts' face."

He pursed his lips and blew out a raspberry. "Being back here isn't easy."

"Have you been to see Amy?" She propped up on an elbow. The lack of response made her frown. "Come here."

"Hm?"

"Come here." She patted the bed next to her and lifted the covers. "Stop pouting like a child and come here."

After a heavy, put-upon sigh he pushed off the chair. He slid into the bed. "What's all this about?"

The moment he got close she turned on her side and backed up until he spooned her. She sighed as he wrapped his arm around her waist and nuzzled her neck. "Better?"

"More than you know."

"Not possible." Every ache eased with him around her. "Now did you go to see Amy? Make sure the site is taken care of?"

"I did. The headstone is clean. The tree we planted is so tall."

"I know." She turned her head when he jerked back in surprise. "Just because I didn't know your sister doesn't mean I don't care. I visit once a month with your mother. Justina and I organize the local walk for Cystic Fibrosis research. I didn't forget how much it meant to you."

"I didn't know." His voice caught and he snuggled close again so she couldn't see him. "I still work with the foundation in the city, too."

"I guessed as much." She closed her eyes when his hand closed over hers. Their fingers laced together and he squeezed tight. Any mention of his sister always brought this reaction. So she let him grieve again.

He'd only been six when Amy had died, back when the Cystic Fibrosis patients' life span had been so much smaller than it was today. Her death had changed Alan's world, and his family's. His dad dealt with the loss through drinking and had never really stopped.

When his grip relaxed enough that she thought it might have passed she turned her shoulders again until their foreheads pressed together.

"I'm worried about Mom." His voice was still tight with grief, and he kept his fingers laced with hers. "How she's going to handle things."

"Dotty is going to be just fine." She extricated her hand from his so she could face him fully. "She and your father have had three years to prepare for this. They've had six more months than the doctors said they would. Not to mention Dotty is a very strong woman."

"She always has been. But when will it be too much?"

Her arms went around him and she kissed his temple as he curled into her. "She still has you. When Sean is gone, she'll still have you. And I'll keep checking on her when you go back to New York. Dotty has a full life. She'll be okay. It's you that I'm worried about, not Dotty."

"I'll be fine. It'll be a relief to have it over."

Pain edged around her worry. She trailed her fingers through his hair, tracing the silver at the temples. "I worry that you won't forgive him before it's too late."

Silence greeted her statement, his face remained buried in her shoulder. She could feel the tickle of his eyelashes as he blinked.

She sighed and placed another kiss to the top of his head. "You'll never guess who found me online last year."

The change in subject relaxed his tight hold on her and the tension drained from his shoulders. "Who would that be?"

"Dolf."

"No way." That proved enough to reenergize him and he propped himself up on his elbow to face her. "Not the Dolf Biermann from 4G."

"Yes. The very same." Out of the sadness of a few minutes ago, they both started to grin. Her cheeks grew tight from her smile. "The one that used to play the accordion every night at three-thirty AM on the dot."

He started to chuckle. "And there was no soundproofing in that place. My God, do you remember that apartment?"

Laughter burst from its seams and she nodded fiercely. "Are you kidding? It was our first home! Not that I'd call it an apartment. It was a postage stamp."

"And we barely scraped by on rent." He nestled into the covers, his hand slipping along her stomach in a familiar and comfortable gesture. "You worked your ass off."

"You had school."

"And you had work and lessons. I still don't know how you did it. Or how you managed to cook anything on that—well, I can't call it a stove."

"It was a glorified hot plate." Her laughter grew so strong tears started to form. "And that landlord. He was such a peeping tom. I swear he bore holes in the walls to look in on his tenants."

"He was so creepy." Alan shook his head. "I hope that guy doesn't still run a building. He's probably figured out how to install those small cameras all over the place."

She shuddered. "Ugh. I wouldn't doubt it. Creepy doesn't begin to cover him."

"Sad that I miss that place sometimes."

"Looking back is always easier. It was a wonderful time in our lives." She sighed and nestled closer against his shoulder. "Back then I never imagined we'd be here. Living separate lives."

"Me either." The laughter faded as quickly as it had arrived. He sighed into her hair. "I never wanted that for us."

"I know." The word caught in her throat, and she fiddled with the edge of the sheet. "I've always known. I told you, I don't blame you. Or me. The fault is neither of ours, and it's both of ours. We didn't give up on our dreams."

"We gave up on us."

* * * *

Around eight in the morning Alan's mom called and said due to the snow, she'd be keeping Justina another night. Something about it being the same bus for school anyway. Alan was pretty sure she was just trying to give him an excuse to stay longer.

All he wanted to do now was run.

Being around Ivy woke up feelings he'd thought long dead. In the rental car sat half of his luggage, as it had since he'd arrived back in Lake Point. He'd wanted the ease of a fast exit if he needed it.

Before he took a shower he'd gone out to get his bag, and now sat staring into it. His wet hair dripped onto the cool tile floor, splashing against the spotless white tile. In the bottom of the bag sat the item he'd brought home with the intent to chuck into Lake Ontario.

He hadn't been able to. On the way into town he'd stopped at a lake-side park and pulled the box out. On the fence with the box in his hand, he'd been ultimately unable to let go.

Then, there Ivy had been.

On that stage, reminding him of the future he'd left behind. The same one held inside that box. He picked up the box and cracked it open again. The single diamond shone back at him, reflecting the bright bathroom lights clearly and brightly.

Ivy had never seen the ring. Never knew it existed.

A knock on the door startled him out of his reverie.

"You still alive in there? Or should I call the Sheriff for a search and rescue party?"

"I'm still here." He chuckled. "I'll be out in a few minutes."

"All right. Coffee's ready. I've got eggs and bacon cooking, so don't be too long."

"You had me at bacon. I'll be right there." He waited a few minutes until he was sure she was out of hearing range before he snapped the box shut. He dropped the ring back into his bag and stood.

His OCD nature would usually make him take care with his suit, but all he wanted to do was hide the ring and what it made him feel. So he shoved his suit into the bag until he almost couldn't shut it. The cleaner could sort out the mess when he got home.

He ran his fingers through his wet hair, spraying little droplets of water over himself and the mat. It wouldn't do to leave her bathroom in worse shape than he'd found it in, not to mention the small mess he made bothered him.

So he took a few minutes to clean up and dry off the room. Once he felt it was acceptable he grabbed his bag and left the room. He knew it would be better to put his bag back in the car, but rather than waste the time, he set it on a chair in the living room as he passed through.

The smell of bacon, and the sight of Ivy in tight jeans and a tighter sweater kept him moving toward the kitchen. "Mmm. Bacon."

"You are such a man."

"You weren't complaining last night."

A smile curved her lips even as a blush rose to her cheeks. She turned to pull the bacon out of the oven. "Of course I didn't. In case you hadn't guessed I've had quite a dry spell going here."

He crossed the room to press against her back when she straightened. She leaned into him so he reached around and grabbed a piece of bacon. With it shoved into his mouth fast, he spoke around it. "Me too."

"I doubt yours has been as long as mine." She slapped his hand with the spatula when he reached for another slice. "Sit down and eat like a grown man. I'll bring you a plate, you impatient fool."

With a laugh he pressed a kiss to her neck, swiping another slice of bacon before she could react. Still chuckling, he sat at the bar again. "I think you'd be surprised."

"Try me."

"Six months."

"Oh. You poor baby." Her lip stuck out in a mocking pout when she dropped his plate on the counter in front of him. "How have you ever survived?"

"That just doesn't sound genuine. It really was painful." The ease of their conversation had returned now that it strayed outside of painful topics for them. "Six months is a long time."

One elegant eyebrow rose and her lips pursed into a taunting little pout. She slid into the chair next to him and set her plate on the counter. Once she'd straightened her napkin in her lap and gathered a forkful of eggs, she spoke. "Try two years."

He froze with a slice of bacon halfway in his mouth. Beside him she still ate, but he couldn't seem to find his stomach again quite yet. "I'm sorry. What?"

"You heard me quite clearly."

"Two years?" He shoved the bacon into his mouth to chew on her revelation for another minute. "I guess I figured you still dated."

"Of course. I do still have a life. I just don't sleep with every man that takes me out to a fancy dinner." She smirked. "You should feel special."

"Usually do around you."

Just as her cheeks started to darken again and her mouth opened for a retort, the sliding door in the kitchen flew open.

"Morning, Ivy! Brought back your—oh. Well." Mary looked like the cat that just ate the canary. "Hello there, Alan. Is that your car in the driveway? I never guessed."

Ivy snorted. She rolled her eyes at him and hopped off her chair. "Good morning, Mary. Here, I'll take that dress. Did it work for you?"

"It sure did. I was a hit at the company party. Frank said to thank you, and I have to thank you, too. It really got his motor revving." Mary eyed Alan with a cockeyed smile. "Get snowed in, Alan?"

He shrugged. "Just visiting a friend, Mary. No need to be crass about it."

"Of course. A friend." Mary leaned on the counter and batted her eyelashes at him like they were still in high school. "Can we expect to see more of you now? I know I certainly won't be disappointed."

"Mary." Ivy snapped. The garment bag got tossed aside. "Why don't you go on home? Alan has no more intention of staying in Lake Point than you do to join a cult."

The words stung a little more than he suspected Ivy intended them to. Immediately he thought of the ring in the next room.

"Well excuse me." Mary sighed and straightened. "I guess I'll head back home. You two stay warm. They're predicting more snow tonight, would hate for you to get cold on all that friendship."

Ivy curled a lip at Mary's departing back. Once the door closed again, she let out a sigh. "Sorry. She must have seen your car in the driveway. She lives two doors down."

"You live two doors down from Mary? That would have been nice to know."

"I thought the snow would keep her away." She disappeared into the closet and emerged with a mop. "Silly me."

"Silly you. Why on earth would you buy this place knowing she lived so close?"

"I didn't." As she cleaned, she avoided his gaze. "I liked the location. The lake within view, the privacy of a cul-de-sac. I didn't think to check who my neighbors were."

"Hindsight."

"You betcha. I still wouldn't pick any other house, though. Save for the nosey neighbor, it's perfect." She finished cleaning up the mess and stowed the mop back in the closet. "I fell in love with it, and still am after some improvements, of course."

"Ivy."

"Maybe you should go."

"What?" He rose and strode over to her side. "Ivy. You don't care about silly rumors, do you?"

"Please. This isn't about Mary." She turned her gaze up toward him. "You're going to leave again. I'd rather you did it sooner than later before we get too comfortable about anything. It'll be easier for all involved."

"What if I don't want easier?" The thought of leaving now tore him up. It hadn't been enough time, enough of Ivy. "We always do it the easy way."

"What else is there?"

"I don't know."

* * * *

Ivy curled her legs up under her, and leaned her elbow on the back of the couch. On the other side of the couch, Alan had the same look he'd had that morning. Even in jeans and a t-shirt he managed to look handsome beyond belief. It had about killed her to tell him to leave, but it had felt so necessary.

All her adult life she'd loved him, and just when she thought she might get over him he waltzed back into her life. She thought she could handle it, but that morning had made it clear that she'd been wrong.

"I don't know what you want me to say." Alan steepled his fingers and leaned his elbows on his knees.

"When will you return to the city?" She picked at her nail rather than look directly at him.

"I'd planned on staying through Christmas." He sighed, his back hunched over as he ran his fingers through his hair. "Unless…"

"You found the perfect excuse to go back sooner."

"Ivy."

"It's okay." She leaned on her hand. "You don't need to lie to me. That part of the story isn't about me. I knew the minute I saw you that you wouldn't be here long. I'm surprised you came at all."

"So am I. But when I saw you, it didn't seem so bad anymore."

Despite herself, she smiled. "Always the charmer."

"Did you really think you weren't enough for me?"

Emotion choked her throat and burned her nose. She closed her eyes against the tears and took a shaky breath. "I don't know. I might have been once. When we lived in that postage stamp."

"For years, you were enough. I thought maybe you needed more." The couch shifted and when she opened her eyes, he'd disappeared into the front room. A few minutes later he was back, hesitating at the dividing line between the rooms.

"How could you ever think that?" She sat taller at his approach. "I wouldn't have had anything I did without you pushing me. Your plans, your goals."

"You did all the work."

"So did you." She smiled and reached over to touch his cheek. "Your goals just never had the time clock mine did."

"That's why I didn't want to hold you back."

"Hold me back? Never. I—" Her words snapped off in a gasp. From behind his back he'd pulled a small box out. It couldn't be what she thought it was.

"When we finally moved out of that small apartment into the bigger one, you remember? I'd graduated and had my first job. We thought we were rolling in the dough."

She couldn't speak, her gaze still fixed on the box. All she could do was nod.

"That's when I started paying on this. Took me almost a year. Just when I finally had it paid for, and ready to show it to you, you got your first role." He set the box in her hand. Small as it was, it felt like a boulder. "I wanted you to have that joy, to be able to really enjoy stepping out of the line. So I waited."

Her hand shook on its way to the lid. With a small *click* the box opened to reveal the ring she'd always hoped for. How many times she'd wished he'd have proposed. Every success they'd celebrated would have paled in comparison.

"Since the accident, your one goal was to be more than one of the flock. You wanted to be the swan. I couldn't take that away from you."

"I wasn't the swan. And this wouldn't have taken away from it." The words felt strangled, tangled up in too much emotion. "This would have made it better. It would have meant so much more."

"Exactly." His hands wrung together. "I couldn't take away from the high of what you were feeling. I wasn't going anywhere. Besides, you were so busy after that. By the time your life slowed down, I got the promotion."

"And I got another role. We didn't see each other for almost three months. We slept next to each other, but you left so early."

"You came home so late."

With a flick of her wrist she closed the box on the simple, yet stunning ring. The exact sort of ring she would have loved. She set the box on the cushion between them with great care. Her eyes burned with tears she didn't want to let fall, even though it seemed so inevitable. "Our careers took us on such different paths."

"I kept waiting for the right time. I thought it would come."

"It was always there."

"I needed it to be perfect."

A short, barking laugh escaped and she flew to her feet. She crossed the room to the picture window. A few tears escaped her weak control. She wiped at the damp trails and swallowed the lump in her throat to avoid sniffling. "It never could be. Look at us. Twenty-some years after we first got together and we still have such different visions of the future."

"Ivy. I can't stand it when you cry." He was behind her already, her attempts to hide her emotions hadn't fooled him. Warm hands settled on her shoulders and pulled her against him.

"I know. That's why I never did. This time, it feels final." Rapid blinks couldn't stop all her tears and another escaped. "It has to be final. I can't cling to you anymore, Alan. I can't keep hoping that you're going to come back into my life and we'll finally be together. I am too old for childish dreams."

"It's not childish."

"Isn't it?"

He turned her to face him. His eyes were red, bloodshot with emotion he couldn't fully hide. "Maybe one day…"

She laughed as best she could and shook her head. "It is one day. We still don't share the same goals. The same dreams. I've loved you for so long. I always thought that at some point in our life we would be able to make it work. That one day we would be enough for each other."

Eyes closed, his hands tightened on her upper arms. One single tear escaped to slip down his cheek.

"I have to let you go. You have to let me go. We can't do this to each other anymore." Words froze up in her throat. Her lip trembled and she wrapped her arms tight around him. With her face buried in his chest, the first sob let loose.

His arms circled her and held her close. "Ivy."

"I love you." She choked out, holding him as tight as she could. "I never stopped loving you."

"I love you too." The words were whispered into her hair, his voice tight and strangled. "I wish—"

"No. No more wishes." She had to get a grip on herself or she'd fall back into the trap. Sniffling against the tears, she pulled back and swiped at them. Her fingers pressed to the bridge of her nose to try to settle them down. "This has to be the last time we walk away from each other. There's nothing else left to wish for."

"Are we really going to do this?"

She pinched her tongue between her teeth, focused on his chest so she wouldn't cave. Every time they'd walked away from each other the past came back to haunt her thoughts. "When we were younger it was easier."

"I don't think we even knew we were doing it."

"Not the first few times."

He rubbed her arms, the physical warmth of the action couldn't touch her heart. "I don't want to lose you."

"We lost each other years ago. You need to go."

His lips pressed to her forehead, and he lingered. "I thought I'd let you go already. This...it shouldn't hurt."

"Please, go. Please." She couldn't take anymore. If he kept talking, kept wishing, she might cave and let herself hope for another ten years.

This time he listened. His hands left her arms, his soft kiss to her forehead grew cool. Rather than watch him leave again, she spun to look out the window. Tears blurred her vision as she listened and waited.

So many times she'd tried to move on. A few times she'd come close. Dated nice men, even loved a few of them. Still, she couldn't deny that when those relationships ended, she'd always had the thought in the back of her mind somewhere that Alan might come back.

She didn't know how to let that thought go, but she knew she had to.

"Goodbye, Ivy." Alan's voice was soft, still strained.

Of course she had to say it back, she needed to say it. The words tangled in the lump in her throat, and refused to come out. She set her hands on the cold window and took a deep and shaky breath.

The front door clicked shut. A few seconds later a car door slammed.

"Goodbye." She whispered before the welling sob wrenched out and she let the emotions flow.

Chapter Five

Alan tapped his finger against his laptop in a rapid beat. The screen held pages of work to be done, but he couldn't focus on any of it. Straight down the hall in his sight-line was the door to the back room. He could hear Justina playing with the pups, her laughter so similar to her mom's ringing out from the partially open door.

To his left was the living room, and just off the living room was the closed door to what had once been an office. Now it was his father's hospice room. Somehow he'd let his mom convince him setting up hospice there would be a good idea.

The door to the room opened and before his mom could catch him staring he turned back to his computer. Work had always soothed him. It should have worked now. But focus was not his friend and the numbers blurred together.

With a sigh, he leaned on his elbow and pinched the bridge of his nose.

"You should talk to her." His mom touched his shoulder briefly. Within another minute he could hear her pulling mugs out of the cabinet.

"Why is Justina still here? I told you the roads aren't bad. You should take her home. Ivy would probably like to have her daughter home."

"I already spoke to Ivy while you were moping in your room. She is fine with Justina staying another night. It's not the first time I've had her here on a school night." Dotty poured two cups of coffee.

"She doesn't want me close to the girl."

"The world doesn't revolve around you, son." She set a mug of coffee next to him. "Just because you're here doesn't mean that Justina can't be. I know you're hurt, but I don't think you're thinking clearly."

He frowned and opened his mouth to retort, but her sad, red-rimmed eyes gave him pause. "It's really over. I have to accept that. I should probably go back to the city now that you have him here."

"Why do you have to accept it?" She ignored the part about him leaving and took a sip of her coffee. "Just because Ivy says?"

"Because Ivy is right. It just makes sense. We want different things out of life."

"It just makes sense." She sighed. "How many times I have heard the two of you say that. I thought you understood by now that love doesn't always make sense. In fact, it's designed not to."

He rubbed his hands over his face. How to make her understand he wasn't sure. His mom had never understood why he and Ivy felt the way they did. The woman had been able to forgive his father for what he'd done, but seemed incapable to understand why Alan and Ivy couldn't manage to get married.

"I really need to figure out how to get Justina that puppy on Christmas without her being any wiser. All the other puppies are going to their homes this week."

The subject change caught him off-guard and he did a double take. "What? Mom, does Ivy know you plan on giving that child a puppy? You can't just spring something like that on her."

"Of course Ivy knows. We just haven't figured out where to hide the puppy until then. With the rest of the litter being adopted, I can't just leave the runt hanging around. Justina might get her hopes up."

"Mom." Alan set his hand on hers. It had taken him all afternoon to rein in his emotions, but they still felt frayed. "I'm not ready to give up what I've got."

"I know an empty apartment and all that money is tough to let go of, son."

"It's more than that. I've got..."

"Goals?" She smiled that knowing smile of hers. "Near as I can tell, you've achieved them. All but one. And you're just going to let that one slip away because you're afraid to come back here and stay."

"I never liked Lake Point. Not since I was a kid, Mom."

"Maybe you need to be an adult to appreciate what it has to offer."

"Mama Dotty!" Justina skipped down the hall, her long brown hair floating up and down as she did.

She skidded to a halt, wide eyes on Alan. With a shy smile, she nodded. "Mr. Alan."

"Good afternoon, Justina." He nodded back, unable to hold back his smile. She really was so much like her mother.

"Is Papa Sean doing better?" Justina turned her attention back to his mom.

"He's still having a bad day, Justina. But he loved the picture you drew for him. You know what he said? He said it would be a darn shame for us to waste this perfectly good snow by staying inside." Dotty smiled. "Why don't we all get bundled up and go out? I bet Alan doesn't remember how good that hill out back is for sledding."

Much as he knew he should work, Alan couldn't help but chuckle. "I used to sled down that thing on an oiled sled. I remember quite well how good it is for sledding. But I have work to do."

Justina's lower lip stuck out. "Aw, but it's Sunday. You're not supposed to work on a Sunday. Why don't you come out and play? I bet you'll last longer than Mama Dotty. She gets cold so fast."

"It's true." Dotty sighed heavily. "This old body can't handle the cold, but I'm sure Alan will last long enough to tire you both out. Why don't you go get ready, Justina?"

Alan leaned over when Justina took off. "Two problems, Mom. One, I don't have snow clothes. And two, Ivy doesn't want me having one on one time with her."

"One, there are perfectly good snow clothes that will fit you in the front hall closet." She waved her finger at him. "And two, she doesn't want Justina getting to know you as Ivy's boyfriend, or as a father figure. I think playing in the snow escapes both of those restrictions. Now stop arguing and get dressed."

He knew he'd lost the battle and his shoulders drooped. "Yes ma'am."

* * * *

For two days Alan had managed to avoid seeing Ivy through a careful and persistent regimen of working all day at the library and spending each evening at his parent's house. Every spare minute was spent helping his mom plan out the financial burden of the next couple of months with hospice care, medical bills, and the household upkeep.

In good news, his mom had been taking care of the bills for the past two years as his dad got sicker, so it was an easy transition. In bad news there were quite a few little details she hadn't thought of.

The end result was that Alan felt he'd accomplished everything he needed to in order to return to the city. After the debacle of yet another one night fling with Ivy, he was starting to feel desperate to return to what was familiar. The rushed pace of his life and all-consuming nature of his job would help him push aside the feelings Ivy had managed to bring up so easily.

He still couldn't believe that for a few hours he'd actually contemplated moving back to Lake Point. Before his mom had pointed it out to him, he'd recognized the fact that he'd accomplished just about all of his goals. All of them but marrying Ivy.

The ring, still tucked into a drawer upstairs, wouldn't leave his thoughts. He liked to think it was just because it was the one unachieved goal. After all, he didn't allow those in his life, so of course it would bother him.

But he was lying to himself. It was the look on her face when she'd seen it. Exactly as he'd imagined it would be for twenty years.

Yet the box had been closed and set aside. She'd shut him out, turned him away. The pain in her voice now haunted his dreams more than her laughter had.

It wouldn't have been right for him to try to move back here. How could he ever be comfortable in Lake Point? In the end they'd split again and this time there'd be a young casualty that didn't deserve that pain any more than Ivy ever had.

Any more than he ever had.

With a sigh, he left his room and hopped down the stairs. The heavenly smell of chicken and dumplings drifted through the living room, and his mom hummed a Christmas carol as she mixed up the cornbread.

"It's about time you came out of hiding." Dotty smiled and poured the batter into a baking dish. "I know what you've been doing. I don't care, but I have to ask you to promise me something, son."

Alan swiped a peppermint patty from the dish on the counter and dropped onto the bench seat at the table. "What do you mean, you know what I've been doing?"

"Ivy hurt you, or you hurt her, or whatever it is you two do to each other—and it gave you a reason to run on back to the city." The oven door slammed and she wiped her hands on her apron. "So go on and run, but promise me you'll be back for Christmas."

"Mom." He sighed and popped the whole patty in his mouth. Rather than glare at her, which he'd get snapped at for, he glared at the wrapper. "I don't know that I can."

"You haven't been home for Christmas for almost fifteen years. Please, grant your old mother this wish? Promise me?"

The tears in her eyes wrenched his heart and he rose fast. He strode across the kitchen and enveloped her in a tight hug. "You're right. I'm sorry, Mom. I'll come back for Christmas." There was a very good chance it was an empty promise, but right then he knew he'd at least try.

"Thank you." She hugged him tight. With a sniff, she extricated herself from his hug and wiped her hands on her skirt again. "Then you'll have no problem taking the puppy with you and bringing it back for Christmas. No better place to hide it than halfway across the state."

"What?" Any sympathy he'd felt moments ago flew away at the quick turn to manipulation his mother had employed. "You mean Justina's puppy? No, Mom."

"I can't have anyone around here take the pup. Justina would find out and want to visit and it just wouldn't work. You have to. Since you'll be back for Christmas, it isn't a problem at all, right?"

It was both a trick to keep him close to Ivy, however indirectly, and to get him back for Christmas. Of course, he could always use trickery of his own to get the dog back in time for the holiday. Still, it was a puppy. "I can't. I work crazy hours, and that dog is so insanely tiny—and didn't you say she named it…"

"Twinkle Toes. Yes. It's a cute name."

"I can't walk a tiny dog through the streets of New York and call it Twinkle Toes. Are you insane?"

"Not man enough to call a dog Twinkle Toes?" Dotty laughed and smacked his hand when he reached for another candy. "You'll ruin your dinner."

He rubbed the back of his hand. "You've gotten nasty in your old age."

"I didn't use a wooden spoon, be glad for that." She chuckled, growing quiet when the door to the hospice room opened. "You heading home, Callie?"

"Yes, ma'am." Distracted by Dotty's greeting, the hospice nurse left the door open. "He's comfortable for now. I think Melissa said she'd be here about nine."

"That's what she told me. Thank you for your help today. I'm sorry he was grouchy." Dotty frowned when Alan slumped back onto the bench rather than take part in the conversation.

"No worries. He cheered up enough this afternoon. Actually, he's awake now if you want to catch him while he's up. Ivy's still in there. I think she's got the magic touch, either that or he just doesn't like me." Callie laughed and swung her scarf around her neck. "See you Sunday."

"See you then." Dotty scooted in front of Alan when he flew to his feet. It wasn't until Callie left that she turned to face him. "Keep your voice down or go close the door."

"Why is she here?" He snarled. "More specifically, why is she visiting with him?"

"Because she has a good heart. She forgave him years ago." The tears were back, but Dotty turned her back on him and stormed back to the stove. "She and Justina both visit with him. There's nothing wrong with that."

"He's a drunk bastard."

"He's your father."

Alan's jaw clenched up tight, and he narrowed his eyes.

"Alan Luke Richards. Don't you dare."

He ignored her and stormed toward the open door, but stopped short several feet away. It had been years since he'd actually seen his father's face. His stomach churned, bile rising as his resolve slipped away and he walked right past the door and leaned on the wall next to it.

Fists clenched at his sides, he dropped his head back against the wall. He could feel his mom's eyes on him from across the room, but didn't budge. Not that he had the slightest clue what he was doing. All he knew was he was furious Ivy would forgive his father after what the man had done.

"Don't give up hope, girlie." The voice of his dad filtered out of the open doorway. Much weaker than he remembered, tired and sad.

"You need to stop worrying about me." Ivy's tone was hushed and he couldn't gauge her mood. The tremble could have been laughter or tears.

"I have to. Don't want to worry about me. Don't dare worry about my Dot."

Dot. How long had it been since Alan had heard his dad use the affectionate nickname for his mom? So many years. Alan closed his eyes against the surge of grief.

"I'll be just fine. And Alan will be too." This time he was sure the quake in Ivy's voice wasn't humor.

"He might be." Sean heaved a heavy sigh, it rattled on the way out. "But he always lived more when he was with you."

"I believe you mean I distracted him from his goals."

"Exactly. He lived."

"I was a distraction. He's happier without it."

Alan jerked forward when Ivy spoke his own thoughts from the past few days aloud. His fist connected with the wall in his frustration and through the crack in the door he saw a flash of auburn hair. Before he had to hear more, he strode to the front door and opened it to soak in some cold air.

"I don't pay to heat the outdoors, so close that door. I didn't raise you in a barn." Dotty called from the kitchen.

The door slammed behind him and he took a deep breath of icy air. It rushed through him and froze the grief into a ball in the pit of his stomach. He hated that she could see through him. Hated it.

She'd said she didn't blame him, but it sure sounded like she did.

Then again, she was also wrong. He wasn't happier without the distraction. He'd thought he was, been convinced of it actually. Seeing her again made him realize everything he was missing. His jaw clenched again and his hands gripped the railing.

The door creaked open before shutting firmly behind him. He turned to see Ivy throwing her scarf around her neck before digging through her purse. With her back to him, it didn't seem like she'd seen him yet.

"What the hell are you doing talking to that bastard?"

A strangled shriek burst out of her and the purse dropped. The contents spewed across the concrete.

She cursed and dropped to her knees. "I was talking to him. I wasn't aware it was a crime to talk to a person."

"After what he did?"

"It was over twenty years ago." Ivy sighed and shoved everything but her keys back into the purse. "Don't you think it's time to forgive him?"

"He almost killed us."

"I know. I was there." She lifted her chin. "I also remember that he also almost died, too. Unlike us, he was in a coma for two months. Six months of rehab. He's been sober since."

Alan snorted. "Sure he has."

"He's tried to apologize to you so many times. It was an accident, Alan."

"He was drunk, and drove us right into a telephone pole. He almost ruined your career."

"And yet he didn't." She lifted the leg that had been broken in the car accident all those years ago. "Fully functional. I had my career. I danced for many years, and I still dance. No permanent damage was done."

"He ruined my chance at a football scholarship."

She scoffed. "Selective memory. You didn't want that scholarship. You wanted to focus on your education, not playing ball. Yes, your knee and back were messed up. Yes, they ruined your chance at a football scholarship, but you already had an academic one so what difference does that make?"

"I don't know how you can forgive him."

"I don't know how you can't."

"He left when Amy died. Disappeared behind that damn bottle and then almost killed me with it. Worse, he could have killed you."

The angry lines in her forehead softened and she stepped closer. Her hand hovered over his arm before she pulled it back. "He made a terrible mistake. I can't imagine the grief he felt when Amy died. I don't want to imagine what it would be like to lose Justina so young."

"You're giving him an excuse. An out."

"No. I'm forgiving him. I don't have a lifetime to forgive him for like you do. I wish you could. I think you should before it's too late."

Alan kept his gaze far from her features, staring at the brightly decorated dwarf spruce trees lining the yard. "Not going to happen."

This time her hand did touch his arm. "Your dad loves you. So much so he was afraid of losing you like he did Amy. In the end, he did lose you because of what he did. Do you really think it doesn't haunt him?"

"It should."

"Don't let it haunt you too, Alan. Please."

"You should go." He refused to look at her. Who knew what would happen if he did. "We said goodbye, remember?"

"I remember all of our goodbyes." When her hand slipped off his arm, the cold air that replaced it seared his flesh. "I don't want you to regret losing your chance to make amends. You'll never forgive yourself."

"Goodbye, Ivy." He ground out through clenched teeth.

"Alan Luke Richards."

That did it. He spun on her, stopping short at the tears he saw on her cheeks. For a minute the anger faded.

Her eyes widened when he stepped toward her and she held up her hands. They hit his chest, but failed to stop him. "Alan."

Ignoring her whispered protest, he claimed her lips. Soft and sweet, their protest faded into warmth and familiarity. He swept his tongue through the familiar planes of her mouth, reveling in the heated return of the gesture she gave.

His fingers wove into her soft auburn locks and held her close until she gasped and pulled back a fraction of an inch.

"Please stop. I told you, I can't do this."

The sparkle of a tear caught his eye and he kissed it away. "I made a lot of mistakes, Ivy."

"You don't make mistakes." She whispered, and her eyes fluttered closed when he continued to keep kissing away her tears.

"I do. I have. I don't want to make another one."

"Then forgive your dad."

Like icy water doused on a fire, she left him cold. He didn't pull his hands away, but he did move back enough to meet her eyes. "I'm not talking about him."

"I know. But I can't talk about this. You can't do this to me. You're going to go away again. You always go away again."

"That isn't fair."

"I did my share of walking away, too." Her hands shook, but she lifted her arms to push his away. "I can't ask you to give up everything for me. That's why I told you that we had to make it the last time."

"You aren't asking."

"And you won't do it. You'll go home to the city and remember why you never wanted to come back here to the place you swore you'd never return. Life will return to normal."

Part of him wondered if she was right. If the minute he got home this need to make things right with her would fade. His hands dropped to his sides and he lowered his head. "What if—"

"I don't want 'if'. And I won't ever be with a man that feels forced into choosing between me and the life he loves." She took his hand in hers and pulled it close to her heart. "Go home. Go back to your life. The only thing I want for you is to be happy."

Right at that moment he had no idea what would make him happy. Something told him a life without her wasn't it. "Happy."

"Yes. Happy." With one step she stood toe to toe with him. She leaned up and brushed her lips across his. "Go home. Please, try to find a way to forgive your dad. And most importantly, find a way to be happy."

Before she could pull away, he tugged her back for one last desperate kiss. With one brief moment where their foreheads pressed together, he let her go. He worked his jaw in tense circles to fight off the sting of tears.

She was right. He had to go home. The one thing he needed was to think clearly and he couldn't do that here. Not with her so close, and his dad right there.

Choices had to be made, although for once in his life he didn't think making a list or a plan was the way to do it. No, this time he had to do what Ivy had done.

He had to take a chance and make a change. It wouldn't take him long to figure out if it was the right one.

First step involved emailing his boss, and confirming his flight home.

And figuring out protocol for taking the damn dog with him.

Chapter Six

Strains of *I'll Be Home for Christmas* filled the silent car. Ivy brushed the tears from her eyes. Every time she thought she'd cried herself dry and that she would once again gain control of her emotions, something triggered them all over again. There was just a week until Christmas and it was turning into a miserable month.

While she'd said goodbye to Alan plenty of times, this time had such finality to it, she struggled to get over it. Then again, her misery seemed to have company. All week long Justina had attempted the silent treatment with frequent slip ups.

"Mom." Justina spoke up from the back seat. She had been just as miserable as Ivy, but for different reasons. The puppy Justina had been begging for, asking Santa for, was now gone from Dotty's pen.

Strangely enough, the puppy left the same day as Alan. Ivy didn't want to think about that part. She took a deep breath and forced the sadness away. "Yes, baby?"

"Are you sad about Twinkle Toes too?" Justina kicked at the back of the passenger seat. Out of the corner of her eye, Ivy caught the flicker of Justina's sparkly shoes catching the street lamp lights.

Being upset about the puppy was far less complicated than the real reasons. Ivy sighed and nodded. "Yes. I guess I am."

"I'm mad. I asked Santa. Santa's supposed to be magic, but Twinkle Toes is gone. I've been good, Mom. It isn't fair."

Ivy pulled into Dotty's driveway and set the car in park. Once again tears blurred her vision, smearing the Christmas lights into large, wavering dots. "I know it doesn't seem fair, baby. But you know what?"

"What?" Justina mumbled in misery.

In the depths of her daughter's misery, Ivy saw a glimmer of hope. She knew that Santa would pull through for Justina. Magic would still exist in her young world, and therefore it would remain a part of Ivy's world. She wiped away her tears and found the smile that had been hiding for the past week. "Santa is many things, Justina. What is he most of all?"

"I dunno." Glittery red toes kicked harder in silent frustration.

"Magic."

The incessant kicking stopped. Silence fell, the soft hum of the engine and whoosh of the heater were all that dared breach the thoughtful quiet.

Ivy turned and reached over the seat to squeeze her daughter's knee. "Santa has some of the best magic in the world. He can bring us our hearts biggest desires, even when we think all hope is lost."

"But someone already took Twinkle Toes." Justina began to relax, although the glimmer of tears still clung to her eyes. "Wouldn't it be mean to take her from them?"

"I suppose it might be, but that doesn't mean you can't still wish for a puppy. You should never stop wishing for magic."

Justina sniffled and pulled her stuffed puppy close. "Okay. I can still wish."

"Always wish. Always hope." It was probably emotional suicide, but Ivy could feel her own sense of hope begin to return. Despite her attempts to quiet the voice in the back of her head that dreamed of Alan coming home again, it sat in its corner of her mind to help her keep warm. She smiled. "Why don't we go in, and you can play with Chester until your friends arrive."

"Okay." Justina perked up and undid her seat belt.

Ivy turned off the car and stepped out, glad Dotty had a neighbor boy that cleared the driveway for her as Justina was already skipping up toward the door. After she'd grabbed the tray of cookies she'd brought, Ivy followed behind.

"Justina." Ivy sighed when Justina went into the house with only a brief knock. She stepped inside and closed the door. "I've told you it's rude to go into even Dotty's house without being invited."

"Sorry." Justina began to mope as she pulled off her coat. Her small brow puckered. "Why's it so quiet? Mama Dotty always plays Christmas music."

Ivy shook her head, stunned by the virtual silence as well. Once she'd taken off her jacket, she held it out to Justina. "Why don't you put these in the closet like Dotty likes and go find Chester. I'll see what Dotty's up to."

Justina nodded and snatched the jackets.

As she started putting them away, Ivy moved through the silent living room with a frown. With only an hour before her Christmas party, Dotty would normally have lit the tree, had a fire in the fireplace and Christmas music going.

Ivy plugged in the tree and flipped the switch for the fire. While Dotty preferred a real wood fire, she'd switched to the gas line when Sean had gotten sick. It was one small way to make her life easier.

On her way to the kitchen, she paused at the door to Sean's hospice room. Only the quiet beep of monitors reached through the door, no murmur of voices. The heart monitor's pace was slow, but steady.

She breathed a sigh of relief and carried the cookies into the kitchen. Preparations for dips and treats spread out on the island, only a few finished plates on the table.

Ivy frowned at the sight. Dotty wouldn't leave her preparations half done. Worry set in, so she went back through to the bottom of the stairs. She could hear Justina already playing in the back room with the dogs. In a brief moment of quiet, a soft sob echoed down from upstairs.

Unsure whether to offer comfort or leave Dotty to collect herself, Ivy froze with one foot on the bottom step. Indecision coursed through her for a minute, until she realized how often Dotty had been there for her in the past eight years. When Ivy's own mother had left town, Dotty had remained like a surrogate in times of crisis.

Without further hesitation, she climbed the steps.

Inside her room, Dotty sat at her vanity. Elbows propped on the table, she slipped a tissue through her fingers and dabbed at tears in between.

"Dotty?"

Dotty started and looked toward the door. "Oh, dear. Ivy. I'm sorry."

"Don't apologize." Ivy walked over and sat next to her on the small bench. Wrapping an arm around her friend, Ivy rubbed her arm gently. "You never have to apologize for being sad. I just wanted to make sure you're all right."

"I will be. I just—it all hit me at once. The house was so quiet. Sean has had a bad day." Dotty dabbed at tears and sniffed. "I wanted to get myself together before the party. I guess I failed."

"The party is still an hour away. You haven't failed." Ivy rested her head against Dotty's. "You have a lot to deal with. No one would have blamed you if you cancelled the part this year, Dotty."

"That's why I have to have it. If I didn't, I would feel worse. It's just been a bad day. Sean hasn't been awake for more than a few minutes at a time. At this point it'll be a miracle if he makes it to Christmas."

"I'm sorry. I'm hoping he does. I'm hoping the magic of Christmas will keep him here for a little longer."

"I hope so too." Dotty straightened. A shaky breath seemed to brace her. "I thought I had convinced Alan to come back for Christmas. He told me today he couldn't. The puppy will come back by carrier. He said he set up a special delivery on Christmas day for Justina."

Ivy's already sore heart bled a little more. She forced up a smile. "I'm sure whatever he does will be pretty special. As long as Justina is happy, that's all that matters."

"I suppose it is." Dotty patted her hand. "Thank you, my dear. You've always been such a help to me."

"And you have been to me too." Ivy kissed her cheek. "I know you're lamenting your messed up make up. While you straighten yourself up I'll get back to work in the kitchen. We'll have a party. There's nothing like close friends and some Christmas cheer to bring about that special Christmas magic."

* * * *

"Slow down, Twink." Alan stumbled when the small dog took off quickly and almost yanked the leash from his relaxed hand. A few curious looks turned his way, but he ignored them.

For the past week he'd done little but care for the dog and spend some time enjoying the city at Christmas time. And little else, certainly not work. Not one suit had been worn, and while at first he'd been uncomfortable outside of his standard uniform, he now felt almost relaxed. Up until now he'd truly forgotten what a real vacation felt like.

He'd even gone so far as to reconnect with a few old friends. Distractions that he'd ignored for years were starting to become pleasant parts of his day. The state of the art entertainment unit he'd bought last year was seeing its first real use too.

After a few days of hard work and dealing with his boss, he managed to get the next six months of his scheduled cleared. Accounts and clients were transferred to his most trusted colleagues, and his secretary had been given a six month vacation on his dollar. For the next six months, at least, he would be on a sabbatical of sorts. Beyond that, he didn't know what would happen.

The thought of his lack of real planning for his future made him a bit uncomfortable. Still, he knew what he had to do, and that involved taking a chance.

Unfortunately, it also meant a heartbreaking phone call to his mom. Something in her voice told him his timing had been worse than expected. He wished he could tell her what he had planned, but he wanted to surprise her as much as Justina.

Twinkle Toes scratched at his jeans and whined.

Alan quirked a brow. "You want me to carry you? You really are testing my manhood, Twink." He bent and scooped up the pup. After double checking he didn't have a mess to clean up, he carried the dog back to his apartment.

"Good evening, Mr. Richards. Twink." George, the doorman, nodded to them as he held open the door. "Good walk this evening?"

"It was, George. Thanks." He crossed the lobby to the elevator. After he'd hit the number for his floor, he scratched the dog behind its ears. "One more week and you'll be in your real home and have a good yard to play in. I promise, it'll be better than this."

Puppy kisses littered his chin with slobber and he screwed his eyes shut. "Nice. Thanks. I really appreciate the slobber."

He chuckled and set her down when they got to his floor. Twink already knew the way and scampered toward the door at the end of her leash.

Once he unlocked the door and tossed the keys in the bowl, he noticed the light blinking on his phone. He'd actually forgotten to take it with him.

He could safely say that was a first. His secretary had often joked that he'd have to have the phone surgically removed from his ear.

Alan unleashed the pup and grabbed his phone. The missed call was from an unfamiliar number, but the area code was for Rochester. His heart leaped into his throat as his first thought went to his dad. Could Sean have died and someone was trying to tell him?

His thumb trembled, but Alan hit the button for voicemail. When Ivy's voice came through the line, his nervous heart started pounding hard, still lodged in his throat.

"Alan." Ivy's voice caught. "I'm not calling for me. It's your mom. I know why you called, why you plan on not coming back. I understand. But please, think hard about this. Dotty needs you. I…"

The line was muffled and he could hear her voice and Justina's talking. She came back on the line again, the doorbell ringing in the background. His parent's doorbell. It must be the night of the party. "Just think about it."

He already had. It took every bit of will power he had not to call Ivy back and tell her the truth. Explain everything, but he couldn't. Not yet.

He did, however, save her phone number in his contacts.

It was a phone number he'd never lose again.

Chapter Seven

The doorbell rang, interrupting Justina in the middle of a bite. Her eyes danced with excitement as she straightened.

"Finish your breakfast." Ivy chided and wagged her finger at the girl. "Once you've eaten everything we can open presents."

Justina sagged and finished putting the bite of French toast in her mouth. While she'd been allowed to open up her stocking, Ivy was making her wait for actual presents until Dotty arrived.

It was the standard yearly tradition for them, but every year it got harder for Justina to comply. This year seemed particularly hard since she'd been hoping for a puppy.

Ivy opened the door with a grin that faded when she found Dotty's brows turned down in worry. "Dotty?"

"I don't know where it is." Dotty whispered as she stepped inside. "Alan swore it would be here for this morning, but I haven't seen it."

"Have you tried calling him? Justina will be so disappointed." Ivy's heart sank. Of all the things she couldn't stand, it was to see her daughter disappointed. "She can hardly eat, she's so excited to tear into her presents."

"I know." Dotty squeezed her arm. "We just have to hope he pulls through. He did say he had a surprise delivery planned for her. Maybe..."

Ivy chewed her lip and nodded. The worry of getting Justina her puppy had been at the forefront for days. She had to have faith that Alan's plan was sound. A laugh bubbled up and she snorted.

"Ivy?"

"I just realized that I'm worrying over a plan of Alan's falling through. Alan never fails to follow through on his plans." Her laughter escaped and Ivy giggled. "I suppose I should stop worrying and let Justina dive in."

Dotty joined in her laughter and nodded. "That sounds like a good idea. You're right about Alan's plans. I guess we should just trust him to see it through."

"How is Sean today?"

"He's having a good day. I don't think I'll be staying long. I'd like to get back and enjoy the time we have." Dotty set her coat on the coat rack and her purse on the floor. When Justina came barreling out of the kitchen, her smile brightened. "Merry Christmas, Justina!"

"Merry Christmas." Justina ran over and hugged Dotty tight. "Can I open presents now, Mom? Can I?"

"Go ahead." Ivy laughed. With a small sigh she followed Justina and Dotty into the living room.

One by one Justina tore through the presents, looking for the elusive dream present. Clothes were tossed aside. Dolls, toys, video games all met the same fate. The family room was coated in a thick layer of wrapping paper and boxes.

Dotty had spent the whole time happily snapping pictures with her camera and now sat laughing at the mess. "I don't remember you being quite so careless before, Justina. What has gotten into you?"

Justina sat quiet, surveying the mess with watery eyes. "I thought…"

The front door burst open.

"Ho Ho Ho." A loud voice rang through the house, cold air drifting in before the door slammed shut.

Ivy flew to her feet in a panic, staring with wide eyes as a man in a Santa suit appeared. While Justina squealed in delight, Ivy moved quicker than her daughter to stand in front of the man.

Warm brown eyes smiled at her and gave her a wink. Her heart stopped and then began to flutter madly. She whispered in a strained voice. "Alan?"

"I heard there was a special wish being made at this house." Santa stepped around her with his pack. "One that required hand delivery."

Ivy blinked against tears, barely turning in time to see him open the pack. A squirming puppy erupted, barking and running through the wrapping paper. She laughed and pressed her fingers against the bridge of her nose to stop the tears when Justina squealed and scrambled after the puppy.

"Mom! Look, its Twinkle Toes." Justina stood up with the puppy squirming in her arms and licking her face. She giggled and set the puppy down, chasing after it again.

With Dotty taking picture after picture, Santa stood up and turned to face Ivy. He moved closer, but then the puppy flew between them and disrupted their tentative approach.

Ivy shook her head, still wiping at tears. "We'll talk soon. I have to do this first."

Santa held out his hand and Ivy gripped it, squeezing tight before wading through the wrapping paper after Justina.

* * * *

Alan sipped his milk through a straw, the uncomfortable beard still stuck on his face. The thought of leaving and changing had crossed his mind several times, but Justina was too excited with the novelty of having Santa there for him to make his escape. Now she plied him with cookies and milk, and he obliged whole-heartedly.

His mom sat next to him when Ivy called Justina over to have her help clean up the mess. "You did a good thing today."

"I hope it's not the only good thing I do." Alan couldn't take his eyes off Ivy, and was pleased that she kept glancing his way too. The smile she'd granted him once she knew who he was had made his day. Now he just had to make sure he still had the guts to say what he wanted to.

"What are your plans?" Dotty took a sip of the wine Ivy had poured for her, then spun the glass on the table. "Will you be staying?"

"I'm not sure yet." He rose when Ivy directed Justina outside with the puppy. "If I'm at Christmas dinner, then you can assume I am here for a while."

Dotty took a deep, shuddering breath. "Thank heavens."

Alan chuckled and left the kitchen. It took over five strides to reach Ivy on the other side of the family room, and that was too long. He set his hand on her elbow, relief hitting him when she spun and wrapped her arms around him tight. "I missed you."

"You big jerk."

Laughter rang out, not the jolly laughter of Santa, but he couldn't stay in character. "I need to talk to you."

She sniffed and glanced out the back door. Just off the patio Justina and the puppy romped through the snow. "She's going to get soaked."

"I'll keep an eye on her." Dotty walked over to the door. "She'll be fine, children have been playing in the snow in inappropriate clothes for years. Let her enjoy the puppy, she'll come in when she's cold and get dressed for dinner. Go on, you two."

Ivy nodded and let Alan lead her from the family room toward the front door. After she'd wiped at a tear, she sighed. "Alan, I don't know what you—"

"Will you let me talk?" He cut her off before she could assume or protest him being there. The past two weeks had been spent trying to figure out what to say. Now all of his preparations flew out the window as he stood there with her.

She wrapped her arms around herself and gave a small nod.

"You told me you wanted me to be happy. How could you ever think that I would ever be happy without you in my life?"

With a jolt she turned her bright green eyes up toward him. "It wasn't an ultimatum."

"Shut up." Alan grinned at the red filling her cheeks. "Do you know what I've spent the past two weeks doing?"

Still wide-eyed, she shook her head.

"I've been taking care of that dog, walking around the city, meeting up with old friends. I've been making a new list of goals, and I haven't worked one day."

Her brow furrowed. "Just because you're home doesn't mean you aren't working. You worked every day you were here."

"I haven't worked. I turned in my work computer at the office and told them I'm taking a sabbatical. I haven't worked." He tucked a finger under her chin.

"The thing that surprises me the most is that I haven't missed it."

One elegant brow rose and she pursed her lips.

"Don't believe me?"

"Not even a little bit."

"It was really strange the first few days, I'll admit. For quite a few years I've not done much else but work. I didn't have anyone to distract me from it like you always did." This time when she blushed she tried to turn away, but he pinched his thumb on her chin to keep her still. "I heard what you told my dad."

"Alan."

"You were only half right. You always were a distraction. The minute you came back into my life last month you became one again." He released his hold on her chin and brushed his gloved fingers along her cheek. "But I'm not happier without you. You were wrong about that."

A single tear trembled at the edge of her lashes. "You achieved so much."

"That's right. I achieved all my goals. All of them, save for one."

She swallowed hard and shook her head. "I won't be pursued because marrying me is a goal you failed to accomplish."

"I love you."

All arguments died on her lips, but they still moved like she wanted to use them.

"I have loved you since the talent show our freshman year." He pulled her close and leaned down.

A chuckle escaped when she flinched away from the beard and then used her hands to press it down. "There are so many mistakes we made. I can't go back and correct them, but I'm asking for a chance. One last chance to make it right."

"But Justina."

"I won't walk away this time. I'm also not asking for you to marry me right now, although I could and mean it with all my heart. That's not fair to Justina, and it's not fair to you. I want to get to know her, and we'll take it slow. I'll do everything I can to not hurt her, or you."

"You'll be giving up everything. For what?"

"You know what I enjoyed when I was here?" He sighed and rested his forehead against hers. "Besides seeing you, of course. I liked helping Mom out with her finances. In this economy I bet I can help more people. I'm going to try out being a financial advisor. I'm still keeping my apartment in the city, so that I can visit when you do, or more often if I need to."

The pink of her tongue appeared pinched between her lips. "Oh, Alan."

"There is nothing that makes me happier than having you around to distract me, to remind me what it's like outside the office. You're the best kind of distraction, you always have been."

She sniffed, fiddling with his beard instead of meeting his eyes.

"I love you. If you truly want me happy, then you'll not force me out of your life."

"Will you stay for dinner?"

"As Santa?"

"No." She smiled softly and finally met his gaze. "As the man that I love."

"Merry Christmas, Ivy."

"Merry Christmas, Santa." She giggled and threw her arms around him. One sharp tug pulled his beard down and she crushed her lips to his.

"Mom? Why are you kissing Santa?"

Chapter Eight

Over dinner Ivy found it difficult to keep from holding Alan's hand. As Santa, he'd made his goodbyes to Justina and left. After about thirty minutes he'd returned dressed in jeans and a sweater. Quite casual for him, and rather handsome as well.

If she was honest, she was terrified of what would happen in the next six months. Part of her feared the next time he'd walk away, certain she wouldn't be able to handle it one more time.

Then he'd look at her and that fear would just fly away. Somehow she knew this time it would work. They had a lot to work out, but they could do it. Now, with nighttime settling in, she felt like just enjoying the moment.

"Mom?" Justina carried over her sleeping puppy and turned on the pout. Big green eyes blinked and she tilted her head just right. If she didn't make it as a dancer, Justina would have no issues being an actress. "Can I stay with Mama Dotty tonight?"

Ivy pursed her lips. The chuckling coming from Alan next to her didn't help in her attempts to hide her own laughter. She'd bet her bottom dollar that this sneak attack had been Dotty's idea. "What does Dotty say about that?"

"She already said yes. Please? She said she'd come back to get me and everything. Said Papa Sean is awake and I can see him. Can I go? Can I?"

"Is she on the phone now?" Ivy tried to hide her grin behind her hand when Justina shook her head. "I see. Is she already on her way?"

Justina nodded, her cheeks turning bright red.

Ivy sucked her lips between her teeth, but nodded. "All right. Put Twinkle Toes in her kennel."

"I want to take her. So she can see her mom again."

"I've got a travel crate." Alan piped up before Ivy could protest. Of course he did, he was the one that drove here with the dog. "I'll get it for you."

"I didn't say yes." Ivy hedged, but then they both stuck out their bottom lip. Tag teaming her already, although she had a feeling Alan wanted the puppy gone so they could have some quiet. She sighed. "Fine. Get the crate. I'd tell you to get your things together, but I'm betting you already have a bag packed."

"We talked about it this morning." Justina grinned. "But Mama Dotty wanted to see how Papa Sean was first."

"Okay. Then when Alan comes back, get Twinkle Toes ready and wait at the door." Ivy sat up and returned the fierce half-hug Justina gave her. "Merry Christmas, baby."

"Merry Christmas!" Justina skipped down the hall. Within a few minutes she could hear the low murmurs of Justina and Alan talking, and the rattle of the crate door.

Ivy sighed and stood, heading to the fridge for leftovers. Already her stomach rumbled at the thought of leftovers. She propped open the fridge, standing when she heard Alan pad into the kitchen.

"Hungry?"

"Famished, actually. Not sure why, you made a good dinner." He leaned on the fridge door. "Mom was pulling in the driveway when we got the pup in the crate. I helped Justina carry it out and got her set up with Mom. She's a sneaky old bird."

"You're telling me." Ivy laughed and stacked up the food bins on top of each other up to her chin. She carted them to the counter, and heard him shut the door behind her.

He slipped behind her and grabbed plates out of the cabinet. "Are you…"

"I don't know." Heat flooded her cheeks when he laughed. They worked easily together to fill up their plates. "I'm just worried that it's too good to be true. That tomorrow you will walk away again."

"I won't."

"I know. This time is different. It's just going to take some getting used to." She stuck her finger in her mouth to suck off some cranberry sauce.

"It's going to take time for all of us." He placed a kiss on her neck. "I haven't been this sure of what I wanted in a long time. I just worry about one thing."

"What's that?"

"Justina."

Ivy turned around and met his gaze. Determined to believe in his surety that he wanted to be there over the worrisome doubt that refused to let go just yet, she thought an explanation was needed before her panic. "How's that?"

"I'm just worried she's going to not like me. She's your life now, and I'm the outsider. It's not going to be easy."

"No, it probably isn't. You two are going to have to get used to each other." She smirked. "And you're going to have to get used to me again."

"And vice versa. Although I have to say that I'm thrilled you're as much of a neat freak as you always were."

"Gee, thanks." She snorted and smacked his chest. "Just for that, you get to clean up this mess before you get to eat."

"Yes, ma'am." With a mock salute, he started to clean up the storage bins and get them back in the fridge.

She carried the plates to the table and dove in, scarfing down her cranberry sauce first. Before she could ask him to hold off on putting that away, the container with the leftover cranberry was set in front of her. "Thanks."

"Some things don't change."

With a big grin, she piled more on her plate. By the time he sat down, she was working on her stuffing. She slowed down enough to be able to speak. "So you really want to do this financial advising?"

"I think so. Of course, my first taste of it was with my mom, so my opinion may be—"

"No, that's not true." She swallowed the food she'd just talked around and took a drink of wine to wash it down. "No, your first client would have been me. You're the one that got me set up with my account years ago. It's your expertise in investing that got it as far as it was, but you taught me how to manage my money early on."

He chewed on that while he finished his bite of food. After a minute he nodded. "I guess you're right. Still, you and my mom aren't exactly a fair sampling of what real clients will be like. So we'll see what happens when I get out there."

"In town, or will you go into Rochester?"

"I'm thinking both. A couple days here in town in a small office, then a few in Rochester as well. I was looking into possibilities to lease when I was in the city, but I want to actually see the offices first hand before I sign anything."

Resting her chin on her hand, she studied him quietly. She was happy to realize she only saw excitement at the prospect of this job. She grinned. "My goodness, Alan. You were wrong."

"Wrong?" His brows knit together and he paused with his wine glass half to his lips. "How exactly was I wrong?"

"You said you'd achieved every goal but marrying me, but that's not right."

"Sure it is."

"No it's not. You wanted to be your own boss."

His eyes grew wide and he grinned. "You're right. I guess I'm getting both."

"You're not getting both yet."

"Oh, but I will."

"You sound sure of yourself." Excitement stirred in her belly. It left her feeling nervous, even though she knew that neither of them were ready for it to happen yet. There was still too much work to do.

"I always am. Aren't you the one that said I always achieve the goals I set my mind to?"

"So you're set on this one, are you?"

"With all my heart."

"Good to know." Pleasant heat flooded her cheeks. She tried to cool it with another sip of wine.

Companionable silence fell between them, and they both ate heartily for a while. The plates started to empty, and Alan cleared his throat.

"I have a favor to ask." He pushed the turkey around on his plate.

The lightness of the earlier conversation dissipated when she saw the tight lines around his lips. She set her hand on his. "Anything."

"I can't make promises. I mean, I don't know what'll happen, but I think I should see my dad."

The last bit of armor she'd wrapped around her heart broke into pieces. Hope went from being hesitant to overwhelming her. Even an attempt to forgive his dad meant he was changing.

"I can't do it alone. Will you go with me?"

"Of course. I'll be there."

"Thank you." His hand clasped hers and he took a shaky breath. "I love you."

"I love you too. I always have."

Epilogue

One Year Later

The Christmas tree lighting was happening in about ten minutes, but Ivy couldn't get Justina to stop chasing Twinkle Toes around the lawn. Ivy chuckled and shook her head, deciding to let her play for another five minutes.

"Still won't give up the game, hm?" Alan's arms wrapped around her waist from behind, and he rested his chin on her shoulder. "You know she spoils that dog."

"She's not the only one." Ivy glanced at him sideways. "You spoil the little beast just as much as Ivy does."

"Guilty as charged." He winked and moved so they could stand arm in arm next to each other. "Mom is going to be sad she missed it this year."

"I know." Ivy sighed. Dotty had decided to take a cruise with an old friend this year, thinking her first Thanksgiving without Sean would be too difficult. Ivy was glad, though, as Dotty had been, that Alan and his dad had managed to find peace before Sean had passed on in February.

Alan had been relieved as well. Once they'd had some time to talk things out, forgiveness had been found.

"So, it's been a year since you showed up at this celebration and saw me again." She kept her gaze on Justina as heat rose to her cheeks. Once Alan had chosen to return home, her whole life had changed once again. "Any regrets?"

"Just one."

Worry hit her heart, but she found comfort in the hint of a teasing tone in his voice. "What would that be?"

"That I didn't come back sooner." He broke into a handsome, crooked grin. "What about you? Any regrets letting me back into your life?"

The past year flew past in her mind. The first six months had been hesitant and careful, knowing that his job still waited for him. The relationship between him and Justina had taken time and hit a few bumps before they started to learn how to handle each other.

After just five months Alan had returned to the city and turned in his resignation. Two months after that he'd moved in with them. It hadn't been a smooth ride, but that didn't matter.

She shook her head. "No regrets. But you were never out of my life. You were always here."

His smile grew warm and he brushed his lips across hers. "We should get Justina. They'll be counting down in a minute."

"I'm right here." Justina rushed up, breathless and holding the still-squirming miniature schnauzer. She blew the bangs off her forehead and smiled. "After this can we go see the lights at the park?"

"That's our Christmas Eve ritual, Justina." Ivy smiled, even as Alan began to protest.

"But we're having new traditions this year. You said." Justina pouted.

It was true. Alan really wanted to show Justina the city all set up for Christmas, show her what it was like in December there. To that end, Ivy planned to take Justina out of school early and they'd go stay at Alan's apartment in the city for a week. The plan was to be back in time for Christmas here, so Justina would be able to see Justin's parents and have a Christmas celebration with them for the first time.

Alan shrugged. "I'm fine with it if you are."

"Okay. Since we're doing new traditions this year." Ivy wrapped an arm around Justina's shoulders when the countdown began. The lights lit up and the warmth of Alan's arm around her waist disappeared. Ivy looked around in confusion, but Alan hadn't moved far.

He knelt on the ground in front of her and Justina. Rather than look at Ivy, his attention focused on Justina. A square black box sat in his hand and he smiled. "Justina. I have a very important question to ask you."

Ivy's heart started to pound and she gasped. Somehow she managed a smile when Justina looked at her curiously.

Alan opened the box to reveal a small necklace with three interwoven hearts, one tiny diamond glittering at the point of each. "You and your mom are very important to me. I know you and I had to work to figure each other out, but you are so special, you made it easy to love you like family."

A lump thickened in Ivy's throat and her heart pounded in her ears so hard she missed whatever it was Alan said next. A deep gulp of air soothed the pounding just in time to hear him ask.

"Would it be all right with you, if I became your stepdad?"

Justina was quiet for a minute, Twinkle Toes struggled in her grasp with little yips. After what seemed an eternity, she turned and set down the puppy and stepped on the leash. She straightened to face Alan. "You're going to marry Mom?"

"She hasn't said yes yet, because I wouldn't ever ask her unless you thought it was okay." Alan smiled and leaned in. "Do you think she'd say yes if I asked?"

Justina's head tilted and then she glanced up at Ivy. A slow smile crossed her features and she nodded fiercely. "She will."

"Oh, good. What about you? Is it okay with you if I ask her?"

Justina touched the necklace and gave a small nod. "I'd like that."

Alan grinned broadly and scooped the necklace out of the box. Once he'd helped her put it on, he turned his attention to Ivy. One hand slipped into his pocket and he pulled out the box she'd seen last year.

Tears cooled on her cheek, and she didn't wait for him to ask, she just started nodding.

"I told you it had to be perfect." He opened the box to reveal the same simple ring, no extra flourish like he'd teased her about the past year. "It took twenty years for me to find the perfect moment. It was too long in some ways, but it wouldn't have been perfect without Justina here."

She clamped her hand over her mouth to cover the sob threatening to escape.

"Will you finally marry me?"

"Yes." It came out as a combination of a laugh and a sob, but she didn't care. The moment the ring slipped on her finger she threw her arms around him and kissed him deeply. When she pulled back, she drew Justina close too.

"How about Christmas?" Alan smirked when she gasped.

"It's only a few weeks away."

"We've waited twenty years. Do you really want to wait longer?"

She laughed and shook her head. "No. Not at all. What do you think, Justina? Should we have the wedding for Christmas?"

"Yes." Justina bounced, and Twinkle Toes joined in the fun. "Can we invite Santa? He came last year."

Ivy laughed and nodded. "Yes, he sure did."

Alan grinned, "Well, maybe not Santa, but we can sure have a wedding."

"A Christmas wedding. Sounds perfect."

The End

Up Next in Lake Point - Deep-Fried Sweethearts

Chapter One

Michaela bent down to pull open the bottom drawer of the file cabinet. As had been her luck in the past few weeks, the damn thing stuck. She jerked once, twice, on the third time it opened fast enough to almost make her fall flat on her ass.

A light tap hit her doorframe before the voice she'd grown to loathe years ago crept up her spine until her nose wrinkled. "Still the best damn view in town. Think it's gotten better, even. You're getting some curves, Mikey."

"Shut up, Gary." She gathered up the game schedules she'd been after and straightened. When she turned, she kicked the drawer shut. "What the hell are you doing in Lake Point?"

"Um, it was just Christmas. What do you think I'm doing here?"

"Trying to con your parents out of some more money in the name of the holiday?"

He slipped into the office without asking permission. While she walked over he had the gall to peer at the papers on her desk. "Don't be silly. I'm just visiting. Thought I'd stay a while."

Michaela slammed her game schedule down on top of the financial papers he'd been leering at. "Cal will be so happy to have something to do, arresting you soon as he gets a chance."

"Aw, come on Mikey. Don't be like that." Gary turned on his charming smile with alarming speed. If she hadn't grown immune the day she realized his many crimes she might have been worried. "I thought you'd be happy to see me."

"You thought wrong. I was *happy* when you left town with your latest flavor of the month three years ago." She leaned on the desk. "We're divorced. You're not welcome in my home, and not in my business, either."

"Public place, baby. I can come and go as I want."

"The restaurant, yes. Not my office. Get out." She pointed to the door to emphasize, but he only smirked. "Don't make me call Cal."

He heaved a dramatic sigh. "You don't have to be like that. I'll go. Just wanted to talk."

"I'm not interested in talking. It's over, and has been over for a long time. Just leave me alone." She dropped into her chair. Rather than give him the satisfaction of replying to his continued griping over her attitude, she started to rifle through the schedule.

It took almost five minutes before she didn't hear him any longer, and was left with just the regular sounds of the shop reaching her ears. She sighed and sank back in her chair. As tired and stressed as she was, the last thing she needed was to have her ex hanging around again. Between his cheating, lying, and drug use, she was more than glad to be rid of him. If only he'd stayed gone.

The pop of a balloon followed by cheers replaced the smile she'd lost with Gary's arrival. Someone just won the balloon and dart game. The first since she'd put it up last week. It turned out to be a lot more popular than the fish bowl game, which surprised her.

Of course, the permanent skee ball game won out every month. She'd never meant to keep it permanent, but it was too popular to get rid of. If she had the room, she'd install a second one.

Another knock disrupted her train of thought. "Excuse me, Miss O'Keefe?" Of course, if her business thoughts had to be disrupted there could be no better way than with Owen Montague, better known simply as Tag. Ten years her junior, he'd grown up into quite a looker.

She could remember joking with her friend, Eve, five years ago about Tag being jail bait for women like them. Now he was legal and even better looking with azure eyes, mussed blond hair and a crooked smile that she bet had melted the panties off of many girls in his class. Just when she realized she'd been staring and jolted out of her reverie, he rewarded her with that grin, and she swore her heart skipped a beat. She shook her head to clear it. "Yes, Tag?"

"I saw your ad. Jake suggested I try for it, I've been looking for something permanent instead of odd jobs." Tag crossed the room and held out some paperwork. "Application, resume, and a few letters of recommendation."

"You want the assistant manager position?" Try though she might, Michaela couldn't keep the doubt from her voice. She flipped through the papers.

"Yes. I'm not in school any longer, I need something full time. Floating odd jobs isn't bad, but I'd like something permanent." He leaned on the desk, and her gaze immediately flew to the flex of muscle in his forearms. "I hope you'll at least look at my resume, you might be surprised."

"Letters from Jake and Eve both?" She pursed her lips. Jake owned the antique shop in town, Past Over, Eve was his manager. "Overkill, don't you think?"

"Can't ever have too many letters of recommendation. Miss Ellery insisted."

She knew if she looked up that damn grin would do her in, so she kept her focus on the papers before her. After she'd flipped through the stack of letters, she set it on the desk. "I'll look this over and we'll meet on Monday for a proper interview. I'll allow you that."

"Thanks, Miss O'Keefe. You won't regret it." He held out his hand. When she responded with her own, his warm hand folded hers in a gentle, but firm handshake.

"Easy, Tag. I haven't given you the job yet." She could swear the heat of his hand traveled up to flood her cheeks. If she did give him the job, it would be rough working alongside such eye candy. Especially with how easily she blushed.

"I know. Let's just say I've got a good feeling."

So do I. Oops, hush your inner voice. She had no doubt she was blushing now, but forced herself to smile and nod. "We'll see if it stays. Monday at nine work for you? I'd like to get it over with before I open for the day."

"Nine sharp. Thanks." He released her hand and ran his hand through his tousled locks. The kid knew he had it going on. Damn him. "See you then."

"See you then." Michaela stood until Tag left the room, and proceeded to drop into her chair with a groan. "I'm so screwed, and I'm going to kill Eve if she sent him here."

It would be tough to turn him down, and not just for his looks. Her quick perusal of his resume had impressed her. An associate's degree in business beat out the lack of a true steady job for several years.

The stack of letters from half the business owners in town worked against her resolve to not hire someone so young. Not age discrimination, but experience.

After her divorce and the hellish two years after, the idea for the business had pulled her out of the hole.

She'd worked hard for two long years to get the plan in place and the financing. Every bit of her heart and soul had been poured into The Midway.

She wasn't sure if she should risk it on an inexperienced young man.

Unfortunately, she couldn't go on like she was, either. The Midway had grown into a successful business in the past year, but she was pulling one-hundred-twenty hour weeks to keep it viable.

She needed the help badly, like yesterday.

Right then her best option was Tag. Young, inexperienced Tag. The rest of her staff was high school students or college students or grandmothers that couldn't, or wouldn't, take on the full time work week an assistant manager position would mean.

The ad she'd placed in her desperation had garnered very few worthwhile candidates.

Then along came Tag.

She wondered if there was a pill that would control blushing. One double-entendre and she'd be done for.

A Note About Cystic Fibrosis

From the Cystic Fibrosis Foundation

The Cystic Fibrosis Foundation: Adding Tomorrows

The Cystic Fibrosis Foundation is the world's leader in the search for a cure for cystic fibrosis (CF). It funds more CF research than any other organization, and nearly every CF drug available today was made possible because of Foundation support.

The Cystic Fibrosis Foundation is a nonprofit donor-supported organization dedicated to attacking cystic fibrosis from every angle. Its focus is to support the development of new drugs to fight the disease, improve the quality of life for those with CF, and ultimately to find a cure.

The Foundation's drug development model has been recognized by Harvard

Business School and by publications such as *Forbes*, *The New Yorker*, and *Bloomberg Businessweek*.

Based in Bethesda, Md., the Foundation funds and accredits a national care center network that has been recognized by the National Institutes of Health as a model of care for a chronic disease.

The Cystic Fibrosis Foundation is one of the most innovative and efficient organizations of its kind and is an accredited charity of the Better Business Bureau's Wise Giving Alliance.

When the Foundation was established in 1955, children with CF rarely lived long enough to attend elementary school. Due in large part to the Foundation's aggressive investments in innovative research and comprehensive care, many people with the disease can now expect to live into their 30s, 40s and beyond.

Research Progress

- In 1989, CF Foundation-supported scientists discovered the defective gene that causes cystic fibrosis — a monumental breakthrough on the road to a cure.

• The Foundation played an integral role in the development and FDA approval of five therapies that are now part of regular treatment regimens for many with CF. The Foundation has a robust pipeline of promising potential drugs that target the disease from every angle.

• In 2012, the FDA approved the groundbreaking drug Kalydeco™, the first drug to treat the underlying cause of CF in a small group of people with the disease. The Foundation also is supporting research that may eventually treat the root cause of the disease in all people living with CF.

While the achievements of the CF Foundation are outstanding, there is still much more to do. Learn more about what the Foundation does to fight cystic fibrosis and how you can get involved at **www.cff.org**.

Sarah Cass

About the Author

Sarah Cass' world is regularly turned upside down by her three special needs kids and loving mate, so she breaks genre barriers; dabbling in horror, straight fiction and urban fantasy. She loves historicals and romance, and characters who are real and flawed, so she writes to understand what makes her fictional people tick. And she lives for a happy ending – eventually. And enough twists to make it look like she enjoys her title of Queen of Trauma Drama a little too much.

An ADD tendency leaves her with a variety of interests that include singing, dancing, crafting, cooking, and being a photographer. She fights through the struggles of the day, knowing the battles are her crucible; she may emerge scarred, but always stronger. The rhythms to her activities drive her words forward, pushing her through the labyrinths of the heart and the nightmares of the mind, driving her to find resolutions to her characters' problems.

While busy creating worlds and characters as real to her as her own family, she leads an active online life with her blog, Redefining Perfect, which gives a real and sometimes raw glimpse into her life and art. You can most often find her popping out her 140 characters in Twitter speak, and on Facebook.

Acknowledgments

Three years ago I received the email that every author wants to receive—the offer of a contract from a publisher.

After doing my due diligence I ended up signing with Secret Cravings Publishing, and thus my Dominion Falls Series first found its way to publication. From that point, I have had two series and one stand-alone novel published with them totaling seventeen books.

In the shaky world of publication, they were a lighthouse and a beacon, guiding me through those chaotic first steps of editing, publishing and promoting.

It was heartbreaking to read that they were closing their doors officially on September 1, 2015. They will be missed as a strong base for writers, and where I learned so much from my editors and the company itself.

Thank you to SCP for all you've done for your authors.

You will be remembered by your authors as a great company to work for.

Books by Sarah Cass

The Tribe Series
The Tribe
The Wolf
The Chief
The Raven

The Dominion Falls Series
Changing Tracks
Derailed
Dark Territory
Runaway Train
Home Signal

The Lake Point Series
Santa, Maybe
Deep-Fried Sweethearts
Stalled Independence
Witch Way
A Thorough Thanksgiving
Eve's New Year
Heartstrings & Hockey Pucks
Luck of the Cowgirl
Stars, Stripes & Motorbikes
Free Falling
Love for Hire

Stand Alone Novels
Masked Hearts
Leap

Divine Roses Ink